A Little Murder Never Hurt Anybody

by Ron Bernas

D1253072

SAMUEL FRENCH

FOUNDED 1830

NEW YORK HOLLYWOOD LONDON TORONTO

SAMUELFRENCH.COM

ISBN 978-0-573-67038-1   Printed in U.S.A.   #13769

IMPORTANT BILLING AND CREDIT REQUIREMENTS

The original production of *A LITTLE MURDER NEVER HURT ANYBODY* was presented January 16, 1991 at the Fries Theatre at the Grosse Pointe War Memorial in Grosse Pointe Farms Michigan under the direction of Michael Trudel.

The cast was as follows:

MATTHEW PERRY	Mike Evans
JULIA PERRY	Jodi Brown
BUNNY PERRY	Robin Bucci
DONALD BAXTER	Jim Rose
BUTTRAM	Marty Bufalini
DETECTIVE PLOTNIK	Clarke Scholes

THE CAST

(In order of appearance)

MATTHEW PERRY - Mid-50s, a man who from birth has had more dollars than sense. He is facing a minor mid-life crisis.

BUTTRAM - 40s-50s, the family butler for many years, though convinced he is above being a butler – at least for this family. He is given to crying jags, and harbors a terrible secret.

JULIA PERRY - Mid-50s, Matthew's wife. A classy, intelligent woman who loves her husband despite his many faults – and is always a step ahead of him.

BUNNY PERRY - Mid 20s, Matthew and Julia's sweet, but dim-witted and deeply shallow daughter.

DONALD - Mid-20s, Bunny's fiancé. He is very earnest, and very much in love with Bunny, despite her lack of savvy.

PLOTNIK - 30s-50s, a witless detective. He was born 40 years too late, and read too many Dashiell Hammett novels. (Yes, he can read, sort of.) He fancies himself a cynical gumshoe, but lacks the savvy to locate, let alone solve, a crime.

THE SET

A simple box set – the Perry family's "Library," though few books are in evidence. French doors, upstage, lead to the outside patio. A door at stage right leads to the rest of the mansion. A less ostentatious door at stage left leads to the kitchen and servant's quarters. The furniture – a desk, a couch, some chairs, end tables, lamps, etc. – and the decorations in the room are expensive and tasteful, reflecting old money.

SYNOPSIS OF SCENES

Act one, scene one: 11:30 p.m. New Year's Eve.

Act one, scene two: Mid-afternoon on a sunny day in June.

Act two, scene one: Early evening on Halloween.

Act two, scene two: 11 p.m. the following New Year's Eve.

COSTUMING

MATTHEW - Everything he wears should reek of taste and wealth. Tuxedos are required for the New Year's Eve scenes; a nice black suit and subdued tie for Act One, Scene Two. For the Halloween scene he should initially be dressed as the Big Bad Wolf after he ate Granny, complete with wolf ears, whiskers, hairy paws, a full-length nightgown and a sleeping bonnet. After he removes the costume, he is in in a white dress shirt and black pants. This will expedite the quick costume change required between the scenes in Act Two.

JULIA - Her taste is simple, but elegant. Classy, bright evening dresses for New Year's Eve; a tasteful black suit for Act One, Scene Two; and a charming representation of Little Red Riding Hood for the Halloween party scene.

BUTTRAM - Tuxedo and tails for the entire show. During the Halloween scene, he should have bunny ears and a cotton tail attached to his outfit.

BUNNY - Very tasteful cocktail wear for the New Year's Eve scenes; casual attire for Act One, Scene Two; and a lady-in-waiting costume for the Halloween scene.

DONALD - Tuxedo for both New Year's Eve scenes; a casual, but preppy outfit for Act One, Scene Two; and a knight's outfit for the Halloween scene, conducive to his rapid costume change between the scenes in Act Two.

PLOTNIK - Trenchcoat over a shabby, baggy suit and a slouch hat for all scenes except the Halloween scene where he is dressed in a white Charlie Chan suit, including a white hat, and dons a Fu Manchu-type mustache.

AUTHOR'S NOTE

A Little Murder Never Hurt Anybody is an homage to the screwball comedies of the 30s and 40s. The audience should never for a moment believe Matthew could actually pull off a murder. This is what is known as a Comedy of Remarriage, where two people who have drifted apart find their way back to each other. In the early scenes, there should be a platonic, brother-sister relationship between Matthew and Julia. They taunt each other and try to zing each other instead of connecting. They should never appear truly mean towards each other. They gradually fall back in love as the play progresses until at the end we see in them what they see in each other.

Scene changes may be made in the sight of the audience by stage hands dressed as maids and butlers.

Biographical Note

Ron Bernas is a journalist working in the Detroit area.

To Bob Schroeder

whose support and inspiration made this possible

and to my mom

ACT ONE

Scene One

(It is the evening of New Year's Eve in the study of the Perry mansion. Seasonal decorations adorn the room.)

(MATTHEW PERRY sits on the sofa working on a crossword puzzle.)

(He is dressed in a tuxedo.)

MATTHEW. *(frustrated with the puzzle, yelling out)* Buttram! *(a pause, then, slightly more irritated)* Buttram! Where are you?

BUTTRAM. *(after a beat, entering casually)* Here, sir.

MATTHEW. What takes you so long when I call you? When I call you, you come running, do you hear?

BUTTRAM. *(calmly, quite relaxed)* Yes, sir, I did.

MATTHEW. Then why aren't you winded? You're fired.

BUTTRAM. Again?

MATTHEW. Yes. Pack your bags and be out of here in ten minutes. And don't expect any severance pay, either.

BUTTRAM. Very well, sir. I'll just go tell the staff that you'll be overseeing them tonight during the party.

MATTHEW. Oh, damn, the party. Okay. You win. You're un-fired. But only until tomorrow. You can stay until after the guests have left and you've cleaned up. And until after tomorrow's breakfast which, as usual, I expect at nine sharp in my bedroom. Then you're fired.

BUTTRAM. Very well, sir. By the way, what was it?

MATTHEW. What was what?

BUTTRAM. The reason you called me in here. Before you fired me.

MATTHEW. I don't remember.

BUTTRAM. Very well. But if you do remember, just call me.

(He exits.)

MATTHEW. *(sits down, looks at his crossword puzzle, then remembers)* Buttram!

BUTTRAM. *(a half-beat, then entering)* Yes sir?

MATTHEW. A five letter word for dolt. Starts with an M.

BUTTRAM. Moron.

MATTHEW. Oh good. That fits.

BUTTRAM. I suspect it does.

MATTHEW. Next, six letters. Hard-hearted blank from Savannah.

(JULIA PERRY enters, and crosses to pour a drink.)

BUTTRAM. *(greeting JULIA)* Mrs. Perry.

MATTHEW. Mrs. Perry isn't from Savannah. Besides, it starts with an H.

JULIA. Try Hannah, cheater.

MATTHEW. Oh, Julia. I didn't see you come in. Anyway I wasn't cheating. I only asked Buttram for one answer. I swear.

(BUTTRAM holds up two fingers to JULIA.)

JULIA. Thank you, Buttram. When the guests arrive, do keep Fifi away from Mrs. Buffington's fur wrap. We don't want a repeat of last year's ugly scene.

BUTTRAM. Certainly. Will you two be making your New Year's resolutions now?

JULIA. I'm afraid so.

BUTTRAM. Make sure I know what they are, so I don't violate any of them.

JULIA. Yes, we will.

BUTTRAM. I am normally fired only once a day. But I can rely on being fired at least twice every New Year's Day – because I have failed to observe a resolution of his that I've been told nothing about.

JULIA. Don't worry. By the evening of New Year's Day, he doesn't remember them himself. On the other hand, mine are always carried out.

BUTTRAM. That's true. I'll go check on the arrangements now.

JULIA. Thank you, dear.

(**BUTTRAM** *exits.*)

Well, let's get this over with.

(*She raises one hand, swearing an oath.*)

I, Julia Jacobson Perry, do hereby swear that by January first of next year, I will have completed reading *Dr. Zhivago*. There. Now, it's your turn.

MATTHEW. No fair. You always pick the easy ones. I could carry out all my resolutions too if I made such easy ones.

JULIA. You don't make easy ones. I'll grant that. Remember that year you vowed to run for Congress?

MATTHEW. How was I supposed to know it wasn't an election year? But I have a little surprise for you this year.

JULIA. I can't wait to hear it.

MATTHEW. You'll have to wait. It's a long story.

JULIA. Condense it. The guests will be here shortly...and speaking of guests, Bunny is bringing her new boyfriend tonight. She's very serious about him, so I want you to be on your best behavior. He may turn out to be our son-in-law.

MATTHEW. Someone wants to marry our Bunny? What's he after?

JULIA. That's not a very nice thing to say.

MATTHEW. Maybe not, but we have to look out for our little girl. She's not the brightest lamp on the street.

JULIA. That's not very nice either. Has it occurred to you that he might actually love her? I've spoken to him on the phone. He seems quite genuine. Now please, dear, your resolution.

MATTHEW. Oh yes. I almost forgot. Sit down, my dear, you'll need your strength.

JULIA. I'm breathless with anticipation.

MATTHEW. You see, it all started seven months ago when Bentworth Bartley's wife Hazel died in that horrible steam curler accident.

JULIA. A tragedy. Poor Hazel. She was such a sweet woman.

MATTHEW. Sweet as the day is long.

JULIA. A sweet, sweet woman. *(a beat)* And probably one of the ugliest creatures God ever made.

MATTHEW. At the club we used to call her Witch Hazel.

JULIA. I was so relieved when Bentworth decided to have a closed-casket funeral.

MATTHEW. It was the funeral home's suggestion.

JULIA. They are professionals.

MATTHEW. Yes. But Bentworth just adored her.

JULIA. I wouldn't have blamed Bentworth if he'd been unfaithful to her.

MATTHEW. The amazing thing is – he wasn't.

JULIA. Really? I thought that's why you men belonged to that club of yours – to keep your little trysts undetected.

MATTHEW. Some do. But Bentworth didn't. And not only was he faithful – they shared a bedroom.

JULIA. You don't mean…

MATTHEW. Yes, and slept in the same bed.

JULIA. Oh, my.

MATTHEW. *(shudders)* Having to wake up to that each morning…

JULIA. He *must* have loved her very much. So – your resolution?

MATTHEW. Oh yes, my resolution. Well, after Hazel died, Bentworth went wild.

JULIA. Poor man. With grief?

MATTHEW. No. With joy. Bentworth has been having fantastic fun since his wife died. He's been to Aruba with his secretary. He spent a month in Paris. He sailed the

Greek Islands with a French maid who spoke no English...And when he isn't traveling he plays golf every day, because he sold his company...

JULIA. Your point being he couldn't have done all of that if Hazel were alive.

MATTHEW. Exactly! And I – I...

(bashful, childlike)

...and I want to have fun too, and I can't do it while *you're* still alive, so my New Year's resolution is to get rid of you.

JULIA. You mean you want a divorce?

MATTHEW. No. I mean I'm going to kill you before the year is out.

JULIA. *(as she would speak to a child)* You're going to kill me?

MATTHEW. Yes, so I can go to Aruba, and Greece, and Paris, like Bentworth.

JULIA. *(amused)* So you're going to kill me.

MATTHEW. Don't take it personally, darling.

JULIA. You're going to kill me?

(She erupts into hysterical laughter.)

Oh, I just can't stand it.

MATTHEW. *(raises one hand, swearing an oath)* I, Matthew Carter Perry the Fourth, do hereby swear that by next New Year's Day, I will have murdered my wife.

(JULIA stops her laughter abruptly, and just as abruptly starts again.)

Now just what in the hell is so funny?

JULIA. Oh, Matthew, darling, I'm sorry. I have this picture of you chopping me into little pieces and scattering me under the floorboards. But of course you wouldn't do that. It's too much work; you'd make Buttram do it.

MATTHEW. That is not funny, Julia.

JULIA. No, darling, it's not. It's hysterical. Sweetheart, if you want me out of the way, why don't you just divorce me?

MATTHEW. Then you'd get half of everything, and I'd have to work, and I wouldn't have time to travel and play golf like I want to. Besides, have you thought of what a divorce would do to Bunny? She's a fragile child; a divorce could seriously harm her.

JULIA. I see what you mean. It's much easier to say, "Mummy's with God in heaven," than it is to say, "Mummy's with Paco in Tijuana."

MATTHEW. Don't be flip about this, Julia. I'm serious. We never spend any time together, what with you and your clubs and charities – and me and my club and my business…When we are together we just get on each other's nerves. It's time one of us did something about it.

JULIA. This *is* doing something, isn't it? Well, dear, how are you going to do it?

MATTHEW. Do what?

JULIA. Kill me.

MATTHEW. Well, I haven't planned it out fully yet, but I will tell you that it is going to have to look like an accident.

JULIA. You could hire someone to break in here on a night when you're at the club and all the servants are off. He could break a few things, steal some jewels and strangle me in my sleep.

MATTHEW. I checked on that. Too many details, and you can't really trust them.

JULIA. Or you could cut the brake cables on my car, and I could go careening off that cliff on the way into town.

MATTHEW. Thanks, dear, but it's my resolution and I want to do the planning. Okay?

JULIA. Certainly. I'm sorry.

MATTHEW. It's all right. Now what about your resolution?

JULIA. I already made one.

MATTHEW. And I told you why it wasn't fair. You have to

make a different one.

JULIA. Why? I'm going to be dead before the year's out!

MATTHEW. I think you should make one. Just for appearances' sake.

JULIA. Well, if it's going to be my last resolution, I should do something I've always wanted to do. I know. I'll vow to have a mad, passionate affair.

MATTHEW. Julia!

JULIA. I'll ask Bitsy to set me up with one of her younger and sexier castoffs.

MATTHEW. Now, Julia, you know you can't do that.

JULIA. You're right. By the time Bitsy's men are cast off, they're no longer young or sexy. They're just – tired. It will have to be somebody she doesn't want to go to bed with.

MATTHEW. That eliminates that resolution.

(There is a knock on the door.)

JULIA. Come in.

BUTTRAM. *(entering)* Guests are arriving, and the valet wants you to pry Miss Bitsy off his neck.

JULIA. Tell him not to worry. Her fangs are all worn out.

BUTTRAM. Very good. But please hurry.

(He exits.)

MATTHEW. You'd think Buttram could distract Bitsy on his own. What do we pay the man for anyway?

JULIA. That's it!

(She raises her hand in the air.)

I, Julia Jacobson Perry, do hereby swear that by next January first, and before I die, I will have made passionate love with Buttram. There. Now let's go greet the guests.

(She exits quickly.)

MATTHEW. Julia! Don't think you're going to get away with this. Come back here and make a proper resolution! Julia!

(He exits. **BUTTRAM** *enters very mysteriously. He sneaks over to the telephone and dials a number.)*

BUTTRAM. Hello. Thank you for waiting, especially tonight...Of course this is Matthew Perry...Yes, it's my allergies acting up again.

(He sneezes loudly into the phone, then, after a short pause:)

Thank you. *(chuckling)* Did you think I was my butler imitating me or something? *(after a pause, chuckling again)* Yes, quite ridiculous. Anyway, I'm calling to okay the deal we discussed earlier. According to my sources the stock is for sale...Yes, same options and prices we agreed upon. Move quickly, though, the offer is being rescinded at midnight...Good. Well, I must be off. I've guests to tend to. Thank you for your help. And Happy New Year to you, too.

*(***BUTTRAM*** *exits stealthily just as* **BUNNY PERRY** *and* **DONALD** *enter from the outside.)*

BUNNY. Oh good, this door's open. It's so cold out there.

DONALD. Not to me, you warmed me with your glow.

BUNNY. Oh, Donald, you always say the nicest things to me.

DONALD. That's because you bring out the nicest things in me.

BUNNY. Donald, I'm so glad you came tonight to meet Mummy and Daddy.

DONALD. And I do so want to meet the two people responsible for creating such a wonderful, beautiful woman.

BUNNY. Who are you talking about?

DONALD. Why you, you silly.

BUNNY. Oh, Donald.

DONALD. So when can I meet them?

BUNNY. Who?

DONALD. Your parents, my dearest.

BUNNY. Oh. Well, Mummy was trying to get Aunt Bitsy off the valet so it might be a while.

DONALD. Oh, was that woman yelling for a crowbar your mother?

BUNNY. Uh-huh.

DONALD. Then I can see where you get your beauty.

BUNNY. And I get my brains from my daddy.

DONALD. Then I can't wait to meet him, too.

*(There is a pause as **DONALD** summons up his courage.)*

Bunny?

BUNNY. Yes, Donald?

DONALD. Bunny, seeing you, tonight, dressed like this, beneath the stars in the moonlight, I can't hold myself back any longer. Bunny?

BUNNY. Yes, Donald?

DONALD. Bunny? Oh, how can I put into words what my heart – and other parts of my body – are telling me?

BUNNY. I don't know, Donald, how?

DONALD. I think maybe like this.

*(He kisses **BUNNY** passionately.)*

BUNNY. Oh, Donald. I felt that all the way to my...belly button! Let's try for the toes.

*(She kisses **DONALD**.)*

DONALD. Why, Bunny! You feel the same way I do.

BUNNY. *(starting to undress)* Then lock the door and we'll play Aunt Bitsy and the valet. You'll have to get on your knees.

DONALD. *(hurriedly trying to put her clothing back on her)* Bunny, no! That's not what I meant! Although that would be nice.

BUNNY. *(resisting his interference, trying to undress)* What did you mean, then?

DONALD. I love you. You're not like the other women I

know. They're bright, and witty and competent. But not you. Your innocence is so rare these days, and it's what has drawn me to you.

BUNNY. *(bewildered)* Exactly. So go lock the door.

DONALD. Bunny, darling, don't you know what I'm asking you?

BUNNY. *(thinking real hard)* Well, you love me…

DONALD. Yes.

BUNNY. And you think I'm the one…

DONALD. I know you are.

BUNNY. And it's not sex?

DONALD. Well, not totally.

BUNNY. Then it's…Oh, Donald I don't know. It's a holiday, I shouldn't have to think.

DONALD. Bunny, I'm asking you to share my life with me. Share the joys, the sorrows, the pains of life. I want you to be with me until the day we are parted only by death.

(He brings a ring out of his pocket. **BUNNY** *still doesn't get it. He places it on* **BUNNY***'s finger. Now she gets it.)*

BUNNY. Donald, you're asking me to marry you!

DONALD. Well?

BUNNY. Well, what?

DONALD. Will you be the mother of my children? Will you grow old with me? Will we be one for all eternity?

BUNNY. Donald, you know I'm not good at guessing games.

DONALD. Bunny, will you be my wife?

BUNNY. Of course, silly. Why didn't you just ask?

DONALD. Oh, Bunny, you've just made me the happiest man in the world.

BUNNY. And I'm the happiest girl. Donald, now that we're engaged, wouldn't you like to…

DONALD. Share it with your parents? Certainly, my dear. We'll tell your parents first, then we'll share our joy with the guests.

BUNNY. *(disappointed)* Okay.

(She picks up the telephone.)

Please tell Buttram to bring my parents into the library.

(She hangs up the phone.)

But honey, what I meant was, now that we're engaged, couldn't we...

(She makes a seductive move.)

DONALD. My love, there's nothing I want more, but shouldn't we wait? That will make it that much sweeter when finally, on our wedding night, we become one!

(They embrace and paw each other.)

Oh. life is too short. I want you, woman!

BUNNY. Now?

DONALD. Now!

BUNNY. Here?

DONALD. Here!

(He flings her to the couch.)

BUNNY. Oh!

(She grabs him, pulling him to her.)

DONALD. Oh!

(They kiss passionately, intertwining on the couch. BUTTRAM, JULIA and MATTHEW enter, unnoticed.)

BUNNY. Darling.

DONALD. Darling.

BUTTRAM. Your parents.

BUNNY & DONALD. *(still impassioned)* My parents. Your parents.

(suddenly realizing)

My parents? Your parents?

(They quickly disentangle.)

BUTTRAM. Yes, your parents.

MATTHEW. Just what are you doing with my daughter, young man?

BUNNY. Should I tell them or should you?

DONALD. Go ahead, my sweet.

BUNNY. Mummy? Daddy? We have some news for you.

MATTHEW. I knew this would happen, I just knew it. Julia, we should have sent her to that convent! We could have…

JULIA. But she's not Catholic!

BUNNY. And I *am* engaged!

JULIA. Engaged? Did you hear that, Matthew? They're going to be married. How wonderful.

DONALD. I love your daughter more than anyone in the world. And I think she feels the same about me, too.

MATTHEW. Well. In that case, congratulations…Love works in mysterious ways.

JULIA. Yes, it does.

BUNNY. *(showing* **BUTTRAM** *the ring)* See, Buttram?

BUTTRAM. *(taking out a jeweler's eyepiece)* Mmm. Nice size. Marquis cut. Good coloration. Lovely setting. Congratulations, my dear. When's the date?

BUNNY. Why Donald, we haven't even discussed a date yet.

DONALD. Why don't we make you a June bride. The most beautiful June bride ever.

BUNNY. But that's only…

(She counts on her fingers.)

…six months away, Donald. There's too much to do to be ready in six months. There's a dress to be designed, and satin to be imported for it. Then it has to be hand beaded with freshwater pearls – I've always loved freshwater pearls. and they have to be fished for…

(pause, scanning her brain)

…and there are gifts to register for, and showers to be thrown, and I'll need a new dress each time, and there's…

DONALD. Bunny, dear, we don't need all of that. We just need each other and your parents and our closest friends.

BUNNY. *(as though* **DONALD** *were stupid)* Right. And of course there's my nails to be done, and we can't set a date until we talk to the club…

MATTHEW. Nonsense, you'll have your wedding right here.

BUNNY. Oh, Daddy, thank you. We'll get married in the entrance hall. I'll look so beautiful coming down the staircase in my gown. And we can put a tent up on the grounds for the orchestra and…

JULIA. We'll work all this out later, dear. Right now, just pick a date.

DONALD. The sooner the better. I wish we could do it tomorrow.

BUNNY. I thought I just explained all that to you!

MATTHEW. *(looking right at* **JULIA***)* Yes. Have it January first. *Next* January first. One year from tomorrow, when all the – plans – have been carefully carried out.

DONALD. Bunny? What do you think?

BUNNY. How wonderful. We can have everyone come for the New Year's eve party, and they can all spend the night.

BUTTRAM. Most of them do anyway, the old sots.

MATTHEW. What?

BUTTRAM. I said it shouldn't be any trouble, we'll set up cots.

(He exits.)

BUNNY. Oh, Donald, I'm so excited. By this time next year, all my dreams will have come true.

MATTHEW. Mine, too.

DONALD. I'll be your husband.

BUNNY. And I'll be buried in wedding presents!

MATTHEW. And that's not all that will be buried.

BUNNY. Let's go tell everyone else.

DONALD. Certainly, my dear.

(**DONALD** and **BUNNY** exit.)

JULIA. Darling, you've got to change your resolution. I have to see Bunny's wedding.

MATTHEW. Well you won't be able to because you won't be around.

JULIA. I promise I'll be good all year. I'll even let Buttram help you with your crossword puzzles.

MATTHEW. No!

JULIA. But you can't kill me this year. I have such a busy year planned!

MATTHEW. You and your clubs, again.

JULIA. It's no worse than you and your clubs. Let's make a deal. Let me see…Bunny's wedding and I'll let you kill me next year with no complaints.

MATTHEW. Getting scared? Even though you don't think I'm smart enough to do it, you're afraid I might get lucky, right?

JULIA. Don't be silly. You couldn't possibly kill me.

MATTHEW. Oh no?

JULIA. No. Now are you going to change your resolution, or will I have to change mine?

MATTHEW. I'm not changing mine. So you can't change yours. That's the rule.

JULIA. But I have to change mine. I just remembered something.

MATTHEW. What?

JULIA. I've already slept with Buttram.

MATTHEW. You what? I don't believe you.

JULIA. Whether you do or don't doesn't interest me. I'm still changing my resolution. And this time you'd better worry.

MATTHEW. Why?

JULIA. Because I, Julia Jacobson Perry, do hereby swear that on January the first of next year I will be alive to see my daughter wed.

MATTHEW. Oh yeah?

JULIA. Yeah.

MATTHEW. We have guests.

JULIA. Then let's go mingle.

MATTHEW. Let's.

(noticing a plate)

Is this your paté or mine?

JULIA. It must be yours. I gave mine to Fifi. I know it gives her fearful flatulence, but it's a special occasion, and she loves paté so.

MATTHEW. Oh, Julia. I really wish for my sake you hadn't done that.

JULIA. What do you mean for your sake.

(A ruckus is heard off.)

What was that?

(yelling out the door)

Buttram, what's happening?

BUTTRAM. *(entering)* The guests are all leaving.

JULIA. Leaving? Why?

BUTTRAM. It seems someone found Fifi dead next to an empty plate, her four paws sticking straight up. The smell of paté was in the air.

(JULIA glares at MATTHEW.)

MATTHEW. Don't look at me. You're the one who gave it to him.

BUTTRAM. Dr. Hawkins thought the paté must have been spoiled. He advised everyone to have their stomachs pumped.

(He exits.)

JULIA. No fair, Matthew! The new year hasn't begun. You can't start ahead of time.

MATTHEW. I can start whenever I want to. It's my resolution. Besides, when I start a big project, I want to get a jump on it.

JULIA. Then maybe you should have started last year, because I intend to keep my resolution!

MATTHEW. And I intend to keep mine.

(The clock starts CHIMING midnight.)

JULIA. Then let the games begin!

*(**JULIA** exits, sweeping out of the room as **MATTHEW** follows, exiting.)*

(lights dimout)

(The clock continues chiming.)

End of Scene One

(With minimal time lapse between scenes stagehands, dressed as maids and houseboys, enter and remove the holiday decorations, substituting flowers.)

(At the 12th chime, fade in to:)

Scene Two

(It is a sunny afternoon six months later, in the study of the Perry mansion. Flowers decorate the room.)

*(**BUNNY** is seated, facing a stack of bridal magazines. She is making notes on a clipboard. Suddenly, she breaks down and cries, just as **DONALD** enters.)*

DONALD. Darling, Buttram told me you were in here. Are you all right? Was the funeral as terrible as you thought it was going to be?

BUNNY. Oh, Donald!

(She puts her head on his shoulder, sobbing.)

DONALD. It's okay. Let it all out. I know it must have been terrible for you seeing her laid out in the casket like that.

BUNNY. Oh, Donald...I'm going to miss Aunt Bitsy so much.

DONALD. There, there. Her death must have been so distressing for you – especially since it's the eighth mysterious death on this estate this year.

BUNNY. It seems like just the other day Aunt Bitsy was sitting right here promising me she'd give us the Waterford crystal we registered for. I wonder if she put it in writing?

DONALD. I wish I could have been with you at the cemetery, but my boss is starting to get suspicious about my asking for all these days off for funerals.

BUNNY. *(breaking down again)* Donald, you know how much I love you and how much I want to marry you, but with everything that's happened since we've been engaged, I think we should call off the wedding.

DONALD. Call it off? Why?

BUNNY. Because all of the wedding guests are dying! This is the seventh time I've had to redo this list...Honestly, I don't know why we ever bothered to fill out the bridal registry if all Mummy and Daddy's friends are going to die on us.

DONALD. Darling, I know you're only saying these things because you've been under a lot of stress lately.

BUNNY. *(again sobbing)* And I have more bad news.

DONALD. What is it, darling?

BUNNY. They stopped making my favorite lipstick color, the one I was going to wear on our wedding day. I tell you, Donald, I think the gods are perspiring against us.

DONALD. Ah, conspiring.

BUNNY. Whatever.

DONALD. Darling, buck up! I know things look bad now, but you can't really want to call off the wedding!

BUNNY. Of course not, darling. I'm sorry. I'm just a little upset.

DONALD. That's perfectly understandable, my dear – with the deaths of Aunt Bitsy and that pool boy coming on the heels of that awful business with the gardener.

BUNNY. Crushed to death beneath that fallen statue of that naked man watering the flowers with his hose.

DONALD. Ah, sweetheart, that's not a hose.

BUNNY. Then what...

(realizing)

Oh!

(realizing, yet again)

Ohhhhh.

DONALD. The tragedy was that *his* death came so soon after the fatal poisoning of your mother's entire garden party...

BUNNY. And they were going to plan the flowers for our wedding...

(She breaks down crying again.)

DONALD. *(hurrying to change the subject)* So, how's the new guest list coming?

BUNNY. Fine, I guess. Considering it's down to only seventeen pages now.

DONALD. Even if there are no guests, it will be a wonderful wedding, because you'll be there and I'll be there.

BUNNY. *(as if he's crazy)* Right.

(more sweetly)

…Darling, while I've got the guest list out and we're making changes…are you positive there's no one in your family you'd like to invite?

DONALD. We've been through this again and again. No, there's no one.

BUNNY. I know you never knew your father, but what about your mother? I'm sure she'd want to be at your wedding.

DONALD. I told you no, darling.

BUNNY. But she's your mother.

DONALD. That's not my fault.

BUNNY. You never talk about her.

DONALD. That's because there's nothing nice to say about her.

BUNNY. But sweetie, I'm marrying into your family, I want to know about her. Please? For me?

DONALD. All right, only for you. My mother left my father before she knew she was pregnant. That's why I never knew him. She told me she left him because she could tell he would never amount to anything. I believe my father must have been a wonderful man, because she despised him so much.

BUNNY. But she must have loved you.

DONALD. She despised me, too. Said I reminded her of him. She was always trying to get rid of me. She used to leave me in restaurants and shopping malls. Once, when I was really young, my mother pasted a stamp on me and shoved me in the mailbox. She was furious when I was still there when she returned later that day.

BUNNY. Oh, Donald, why?

DONALD. Insufficient postage.

BUNNY. Oh, darling.

DONALD. I won a scholarship to college, and during my first semester she moved and left no forwarding address.

BUNNY. How terrible, darling. But we don't need her. I'll be your mother...and your father. Only I won't be mean like your mother. And I'm probably a little shorter than your father, and he's a man. So I guess I won't be anything like your mother or your father. But you know what I mean.

DONALD. Yes, my dear, now you know why I love you so much.

(They kiss.)

I've always dreamed of finding my father, but because he never knew my mother was pregnant, he doesn't know I exist. I only have this to remember him by.

(He produces a cuff link from his pocket.)

My mother showed it to me one day when she was cleaning out her dresser. She said it was my father's. She had given him a pair of gold cuff links on their wedding night. It was when she discovered he couldn't pay for them that she left him...She said she was saving this to hock for a rainy day. I stole it when I went off to school.

BUNNY. What ever happened to the matching cuff link?

DONALD. She had probably already pawned it by the time she showed me this one. Some day I'll hire a detective and use this to find my...

BUNNY. *(interrupting)* A detective! ...Oh my gosh.

DONALD. What?

BUNNY. I forgot. That detective, that Plotnik man, is coming over again today.

DONALD. That annoying man from the police? Is he still bothering you, darling?

BUNNY. How can he bother me? I never know what he's saying. He's always talking about dames and broads and people slipping each other dickeys.

DONALD. Ah, mickeys.

BUNNY. Whoever. Anyway, I never know what he's saying so I just smile and nod my head a lot. I learned that trick in school.

DONALD. Still and all, darling, you shouldn't have to put up with that man.

BUNNY. I really wish he didn't have to come over today. I'm kind of stressed out.

DONALD. Well, maybe we can go to our jeweler's appointment early so we don't have to see him.

BUTTRAM. *(entering)* That idiot who calls himself a detective is here. Shall I show him in?

PLOTNIK. *(entering, pushing roughly past* **BUTTRAM**, *acting very "Sam Spade")* Thought you could ditch me, eh, penguin?

BUTTRAM. No, I simply thought you would have enough decency to wait in the hall until I could tell Miss Bunny you're here.

PLOTNIK. Sure, bud, sure.

BUTTRAM. I wasn't sure she's up to answering questions today. Miss Bitsy was her aunt, you know.

PLOTNIK. That's exactly why I'm here.

> *(to* **BUNNY***)*

> Well, what do you say? You remember your old pal Plotnik, here don't you? Are you up to answering questions today, sister?

BUNNY. Donald, every time I see him he calls me that. Please tell me we're not related.

DONALD. I'm sure you're not, dear.

BUNNY. Oh, thank God. Are you here about Aunt Bitsy's death?

PLOTNIK. I didn't come here to watch you two dance around the May Pole.

BUNNY. But we weren't. We were just talk...

DONALD. He means yes, dear.

BUNNY. Oh.

PLOTNIK. I thought you might be able to shine a little light on the matter.

DONALD. I'm sure she can't…

BUTTRAM. *(under his breath)* Because her light is so dim.

DONALD. Please take it easy. She was very attached to her aunt.

BUTTRAM. Who wasn't?

PLOTNIK. Don't you worry, college boy, I'll go easy on her.

> *(to* **BUNNY**)

> Where were you when your aunt and the pool boy bit the dust?

> *(***BUNNY** *looks imploringly at* **DONALD**.*)*

DONALD. He means, where were you when they *passed on?*

> *(She continues to look at* **DONALD** *helplessly.)*

> Where were you when they *died,* Bunny?

BUNNY. Oh. I was at the store registering for my bridal shower. And I found the nicest china pattern, it's got these cute little roses all around the border…

PLOTNIK. And there's someone who could verify that for you?

BUNNY. Yes! I have a picture of the pattern right here!

DONALD. Not the china, dear. I can verify we were at the store, Detective.

PLOTNIK. Aha. It sure is convenient how your stories coincide. What about you, pal? Butlers always do it.

BUTTRAM. Well, this one didn't.

PLOTNIK. How do I know that?

BUTTRAM. Because I said so.

PLOTNIK. Oh you're good. Real good. But I got my eye on you. And on you two, too.

DONALD. Well that's just fine, Detective, because we have nothing to hide. And if you don't need us anymore, I'd like to go for a walk with my fiancée.

PLOTNIK. Stay on the grounds, I might need you later.

(**BUNNY** *and* **DONALD** *exit.*)

That is one hot dame. What's she hanging around with a suit like that for?

BUTTRAM. It appears he actually loves her.

PLOTNIK. Yeah – and her money.

BUTTRAM. I don't know what you're insinuating, but he's a rising star in a prestigious law firm…

PLOTNIK. Oh, he's an ambulance chaser, eh?

BUTTRAM. No, I believe he's a corporate lawyer.

PLOTNIK. So, he's a shyster.

BUTTRAM. No, he's not. He's a…

(*He fumbles for another word, but can't find one.*)

…yes, he's a shyster.

PLOTNIK. And you don't think it's interesting that all these people have been bumped off since New Year's eve, the very day he turned up on your doorstep with a ring through missy's nose?

BUTTRAM. No, it's on her finger. And no, I have never associated Donald with the deaths.

PLOTNIK. That's why I'm the detective, and you serve me drinks.

BUTTRAM. Speaking of serving, I have to tend to my staff. I'll show you out.

PLOTNIK. Not so fast. I'm waiting for the Perrys. The old birds I mean.

BUTTRAM. Then please, make yourself at home. Shall I get you a drink?

PLOTNIK. I don't think so. I'll go out by the pool and have a look-see where the latest accidents happened.

BUTTRAM. Fine. I'll let you know when the old birds arrive.

PLOTNIK. Do that. And by the way, don't get any ideas about leaving the house. I may have some more questions for you. And you'd better have answers.

BUTTRAM. Detective, I always have answers.

(**PLOTNIK** *appears to exit to the veranda, but hides from* **BUTTRAM** *behind the curtains.* **BUTTRAM** *picks up the telephone and dials.* **PLOTNIK** *peers from behind the curtain.*)

Hello, is he in? It's Matthew Perry...Bill, sorry I didn't get right back to you, we had an emergency here...Yes, you're right, they've been dropping off like flies...Oh, dinner is off again this week? Julia will be disappointed. You've canceled every week since that incident with the flower committee and the chamomile tea. Well, maybe next week...

Yes, I'll inform that "idiot houseman" of mine. It's Buttram, not Butt-ram...Say, Bill, remember that little transaction we talked about last week? Well, I think the time is right to make that move. I trust you can handle all the details without me. Good. And Bill, as always, mum's the word.

(*As* **BUTTRAM** *hangs up,* **PLOTNIK** *exits silently.* **MATTHEW** *and* **JULIA** *enter, not having noticed* **PLOTNIK**.)

(**MATTHEW** *and* **JULIA** *are dressed in black.*)

MATTHEW. Oh, hello, Buttram.

BUTTRAM. Good afternoon. How was the funeral?

MATTHEW. Nice, really, very nice. Much nicer than the gardener's.

JULIA. Well, after all, it should have been nicer – it was Bitsy's.

MATTHEW. And that pool boy's too. I had no idea they were so close.

JULIA. It was in her will that they share their eternal rest together.

MATTHEW. But in the same casket?

JULIA. It seemed fitting – their dying together – but being electrocuted is such a jolting way to go.

(*pause, reminiscing*)

Every Tuesday morning Bitsy and I would watch him scrub the pool in his little bathing suit – his tanned muscles glistening with sweat as he moved his hips to that soul music on his radio…Bitsy used to say, "He's so hunk I'd crawl through a mile of broken glass just to…"

(pause)

Oh, never mind, you get the idea…His long blond hair was what did it for her…It's a good thing she couldn't see him today, his hair all kinked up in tiny curls…Oh, I do need a rest. Funerals always leave me so lifeless.

BUTTRAM. Well don't get too comfortable, that detective is here again.

MATTHEW AND JULIA. Oh, God. Not again.

BUTTRAM. Yes. Again. He's out by the pool looking for clues. I'll keep him away from you as long as possible.

JULIA. Thank you, please do.

(BUTTRAM exits. MATTHEW pours himself a drink.)

Make me one, too, dear.

(He pours her a drink from a separate container which is obviously poisoned.)

It isn't poisoned, is it? I'm really not up to dodging murder attempts today.

MATTHEW. My dear, really. Would I kill you on the day your best friend was buried?

JULIA. I'm sorry, dear.

(She takes the drink but doesn't drink it. Several times during the following, until she finally pours the drink out, JULIA puts it to her lips then takes it away before she drinks any of it. Each time the glass gets close to her lips, MATTHEW leans forward in anticipation, and each time she takes it away, he's disappointed.)

MATTHEW. You know I still can't figure it out.

JULIA. What's that dear?

MATTHEW. How the pool boy ended up getting electrocuted instead of you.

JULIA. I haven't quite figured it out myself.

MATTHEW. I took great pains in setting this up so finally *you* would die – and *not* someone else, like the last few times.

JULIA. Yes, it was careless of you to poison my *entire* garden club.

MATTHEW. I meant to kill only you, darling. That you think I'd murder anyone else on purpose hurts me.

JULIA. I apologize, dear. But about the gardener…

MATTHEW. I assure you, that falling statue was meant only for you.

JULIA. Don't forget Fifi.

MATTHEW. I'm not counting Fifi.

JULIA. Why not, you killed him?

MATTHEW. I did not. You're the one who gave him the poisoned paté.

JULIA. But you're the one who put the poison in the paté… Have you noticed, darling, how you favor poison? Somewhat old-fashioned, but you were always a romantic at heart.

MATTHEW. You're right. I've been too fixated on poison. That's why I tried the radio.

JULIA. The radio…?

MATTHEW. Yes, the radio. I got the idea from doing my crossword puzzles. The clue was "don't mix with water." Mummy would always get upset with Daddy when he took the radio into the hot tub so he could listen to the stock reports.

JULIA. Because he might be shocked in more ways than one.

MATTHEW. Right. And then I thought – we have a pool and that you use that pool every morning…

JULIA. Except Tuesday.

MATTHEW. Well, If I'd known *that*...Anyway, I knew there were electric lights around the pool. So I made a cut in the cord of one of the lights, see, and then I put that part over the edge of the pool.

JULIA. So when I went swimming I would turn on the pool lights and fry. I see. Only I didn't swim that day.

MATTHEW. No, you didn't.

JULIA. And poor Dirk jumped in for the pool's monthly algae scraping and...

MATTHEW. Exactly. If you had gone swimming that morning like you always do, Bitsy would still be alive and I'd be on my way to Aruba right now. Honestly, Julia, you should take the blame.

JULIA. Well I won't, because if you ever paid attention, you'd know I don't go swimming on Tuesdays until after the pool boy comes, and after Bitsy and I have lunch.

MATTHEW. Since when?

JULIA. Since we had the pool put in.

MATTHEW. All that time? Really? Well, Tuesdays are my golf days. How would I know what you do when I'm gone? And that reminds me. I've got to get to the club. The boys were nice enough to postpone our regular tee-off time so I could attend the funeral with you, and I don't want to keep them waiting any longer.

JULIA. Yes, that would be rude.

MATTHEW. *(preparing to leave)* Well, I'll be off then.

JULIA. Not just yet, darling.

MATTHEW. What is it now?

JULIA. You know how I hate to keep you from your pressing plans, but you aren't going anywhere until we make new plans for my funeral.

MATTHEW. We've already made new plans your funeral three times. I think that's enough.

JULIA. But we must change them again. Bitsy was to sing at my funeral and she can't do that now, can she?...Such a waste. Thank God Bitsy wasn't in the pool with Dirk, then you would have zapped her, too.

MATTHEW. The doctor said Bitsy died of some gastro-intestinal thing.

(sheepishly)

It must have been the chicken salad.

JULIA. What did you do to my chicken salad?

MATTHEW. I didn't know Bitsy was coming for lunch and I...

JULIA. You poisoned my chicken salad? You could have killed me!

MATTHEW. Isn't that the point? Why didn't you eat it?

JULIA. I wasn't hungry. Bitsy said it was good, though. She took some out to Dirk for him to taste, but before he could lick her fingers...Oh, God, I hope there's none left!...We don't need any more suspicious deaths around here. Soon we won't have any friends left.

(JULIA rings for BUTTRAM.)

MATTHEW. There, there, dear. It's all right. Have your drink.

JULIA. I can't believe you were so careless as to kill Dirk and Bitsy on the same day.

MATTHEW. Go ahead. Drink. I made it strong, just the way you like it.

(As he glances away she dumps the drink into a plant which promptly dies.)

JULIA. Darling, could I have another one please?

MATTHEW. You finished the last one?

JULIA. Yes, and it's been such a long day I'll need another.

MATTHEW. You're sure you drank it?

JULIA. Mm-hmm.

MATTHEW. Every drop?

JULIA. Yes, darling. Now please get me another one. And why don't you join me, too.

MATTHEW. Yes. I think I shall. But...

(*He holds up an empty carafe.*)

I'll have to get some more.

JULIA. Buttram can do it.

MATTHEW. Oh, no, no, no. I'll get it. I'm sure he's busy.

(**MATTHEW** *exits. As* **JULIA** *puts the dead plant outside,* **BUTTRAM** *enters carrying a cardboard box.*)

JULIA. Oh Buttram, you must go immediately, and throw out any chicken salad left over from Bitsy's and my lunch the other day.

BUTTRAM. There's no need to rush, ma'am. We didn't serve you the chicken salad. You see, cook left it out and it was so hot that day I was afraid it was spoiled so I threw it out. Cook served shrimp salad with fresh mushrooms instead.

JULIA. He did? How wonderful! Oh, don't mention the shrimp salad to Mr. Perry.

BUTTRAM. As you say, ma'am. Anyway, your husband's videotapes have arrived.

JULIA. Videotapes? Let's see...

(*She reads the titles with amusement as she unpacks the box.*)

"Dial M for Murder," "Rear Window," "Suspicion," "How to Murder Your Wife"...

(*examining a final video with surprise*)

"Teenage Vampire Sluts?"

BUTTRAM. Oh, that's mine, ma'am.

JULIA. Really, Buttram, you shouldn't have to resort to this sort of thing.

BUTTRAM. No, ma'am.

JULIA. A fascination with the occult can be dangerous.

BUTTRAM. The, uh, occult. Yes, of course. But the truth is, ma'am, I'm a desperate man. The life of a butler is a lonely one. A proper butler must make sacrifices. Sacrifices that perhaps might have been made at too great a cost. To think I gave up everything for this! To think that for this I lost my – my...

(He suddenly breaks down and throws himself into JULIA'*s arms.)*

Oh, Estelle, why did you leave me? Why?

*(*DONALD *enters as* JULIA *comforts* BUTTRAM, *embracing him.)*

My love! My only love!

JULIA. Oh, Buttram!

*(*DONALD *does a double take and quickly exits.)*

What is troubling you?

BUTTRAM. *(pulling himself together)* Oh, ma'am. I'm so sorry, but sometimes the shame of what's happened is just so...Oh, I can't discuss it any further. I must go.

(He starts for the door, but returns for his tape, then heads for the door, bumping into DONALD *as* DONALD *reenters.)*

DONALD. Have...Oh, excuse me.

*(*BUTTRAM *exits.)*

JULIA. What is it, Donald?

DONALD. It seems I've lost Bunny. Did she come this way?

JULIA. No, dear. But when you find her, tell her I need to speak to her immediately.

DONALD. I'll tell her.

*(*DONALD *exits as* MATTHEW *enters with a tray with two glasses on it. He sets the tray on the coffee table, then sits on the couch.)*

MATTHEW. *(handing* JULIA *a drink)* Here you are, dear. Drink up.

JULIA. Your movies came.

MATTHEW. My movies?

JULIA. They're over there, on the desk.

(He turns and she switches drinks, which he notices.)

I see you're running out of ideas.

MATTHEW. No, no. These movies are more for inspiration. I've called the club and canceled so we can have the whole afternoon together. We'll plan your funeral…. That should be more fun than listening to Bentworth Bartley brag about his latest trip. Tibet, this time…. I do wish you would be more cooperative – so I could go with him.

JULIA. Sorry dear. I'll try harder. But it's your resolution, not mine.

(JULIA *starts to drink from her glass.*)

MATTHEW. Julia, you'll need some paper to make the plans. I think there's some in the desk.

JULIA. Would you get me some, dear?

(*She puts her drink down, and looks toward the desk, whereupon he switches the glasses, which she notices.*)

Oh, and darling, this pen doesn't work. Could you get another one?

(*While* MATTHEW *rises,* JULIA *switches.*)

MATTHEW. Of course, dear.

JULIA. My biggest problem in planning is not knowing when. If I knew when I was going to be buried I'd know what to wear. But since I don't know, I'll have to choose three outfits. If you get me before Labor Day, I would like to be buried in that peach suit. Bunny will know which one.

MATTHEW. (*looking over* JULIA's *shoulder*) What was that?

(*She turns, and he switches glasses.*)

I'm sorry, I thought I heard something. What were you saying?

JULIA. I was saying that if I'm dead by Labor Day, I…

(*looking out the veranda window*)

Is there someone out there?

(MATTHEW *turns. She picks up the glasses and sets them back down without switching them.*)

MATTHEW. No, but isn't that Inspector Plotnik coming this way?

(He switches glasses, giving himself the poisoned one.)

We can't afford to make him suspicious. He's already so…

JULIA. He's seen too many old movies is what his problem is. Speaking of movies, don't forget to put the videotapes away.

(She grabs her glass and holds it.)

Do you think those videotapes will give you any ideas?

MATTHEW. They might.

JULIA. Good. I'd hate to think I'd be killed in an unimaginative way like, say, poison in a drink or something. Oh, but even you would never be so passé as to poison my drink.

MATTHEW. Really, Julia, give me some credit.

JULIA. I can't believe *anyone* would be so – *plebeian* – as to poison a drink.

MATTHEW. All right already. Shut up and drink.

PLOTNIK. *(entering through the veranda door)* Hello there.

MATTHEW & JULIA. Hello, Detective Plotnik.

PLOTNIK. I've just come from the pool and I'm very suspicious. Yes. Very suspicious indeed.

MATTHEW. What did you find?

PLOTNIK. I found…absolutely nothing.

MATTHEW. Why is that suspicious?

PLOTNIK. Because most murderers leave something behind, a cigarette butt, a nail file, a family photograph, something. But there was nothing there at all. Don't you find that suspicious?

MATTHEW. No, not really.

PLOTNIK. That's why I'm the detective and you're a nit. Let me tell you a little story. Was this case once, see, back when I was a cub. A bird comes into my office. She says her old man's took a powder with some stripper taking all their dough with them. But this dame wants him back. I tells her I'll cast an eyeball over at the Bump and Grind where the stripper used to shake her willies. Well, before I can do that, the old goat floats up in the river with a frog-sticker in the old pumper. Well I haul in his old ball and chain – a right pretty blonde doe-eye. But she says she was playing sheet tag with her hubby's business partner –what's good for the goose, you know? So I follow up with the business partner who says they were, in fact, doing the horizontal bop at the time of the murder. He also says the hubby is doing to the books the same thing he's doing to the stripper. And when I find the stripper, she sings like a bird and says he left her the day before he was offed. But she was working when he was stuck. So I got three suspects and three alibis. But I cracked it wide open. The old guy was iced by some jazzed-up dopehead needing some gidas for a score.

MATTHEW. What the hell did he just say?

JULIA. I haven't the faintest idea. Well, Detective. Now what?

PLOTNIK. You offer me a drink. It's a thirsty day.

JULIA. Here, have mine.

MATTHEW. *(rushing across the room to grab the glass)* NO!

JULIA. Why not, darling?

MATTHEW. Um, well, because it's warm now. I'll get us some fresh glasses.

JULIA. Stay here, dear. Let Buttram get it.

MATTHEW. *(gathering the glasses)* Oh, no. I'm sure he's too busy. I'll be right back.

JULIA. Oh, Matthew, darling…I think your drink is a bit warm, too.

MATTHEW. What are you talking about?

JULIA. I wouldn't drink your drink. It might not agree with you.

MATTHEW. *(finally understanding and annoyed at being tricked)* Damnation, Julia! You don't make it easy. Not easy at all!

(He exits.)

PLOTNIK. *(picking up one of the video tapes)* "How To Murder Your Wife" Very interesting. Whose is this?

(DONALD and BUNNY enter from the veranda. BUNNY is carrying a radio with an electric cord.)

JULIA. Uh, Buttram ordered them. Oh, Bunny, Donald. I think Detective Plotnik is about to rule that your Aunt Bitsy died of natural causes.

PLOTNIK. Maybe I will, maybe I won't.

DONALD. What do you mean maybe?

PLOTNIK. Just what I said.

JULIA. But Detective, you just said you found...

PLOTNIK. I know what I said, sister.

BUNNY. Mummy? You're not his...

JULIA. No, dear.

DONALD. Detective, just what did you find?

JULIA. Why don't you show him, Detective?

PLOTNIK. How can I show him nothing?

JULIA. Try.

(As PLOTNIK shrugs hopelessly, he and DONALD exit to the outside.)

Bunny?

BUNNY. Yes, Mummy?

JULIA. Remember the other day when we were walking over by the pool and we noticed the electric cord on the light was cut?

BUNNY. No.

JULIA. Well do you remember that we put that light in the poolhouse so no one would be electrocuted when the water touched it?

BUNNY. No.

JULIA. Let's keep it that way, okay?

BUNNY. Whatever you say, Mummy.

JULIA. Bunny, what's that you're holding?

BUNNY. *(as if JULIA is an idiot)* A radio. And they say I'm the dumb one.

(She hands it to JULIA.*)*

Someone left it in the pool.

DONALD. *(entering from the outside, obviously upset)* Bunny, let's go. I have no desire to be anywhere near that detective.

JULIA. My dear, what's wrong?

*(***PLOTNIK** *enters from the veranda.)*

DONALD. He had the gall to tell me I'm under suspicion for the deaths that have been going on around here.

PLOTNIK. Am I the only one around here who thinks it's mighty strange that all these "accidents" have taken place since he first showed up?

JULIA. I can assure you Donald had nothing to do with these deaths, Detective.

PLOTNIK. *(to* JULIA*)* And you're not being completely over-looked. You're always nearby when one more dies.

BUNNY. But Mummy's not...

PLOTNIK. And don't think you're off the hook, either.

BUNNY. Me? Why me?

PLOTNIK. I don't trust anyone with a name like Bunny. And while we're on names, how come Buttram only has one?

*(***MATTHEW** *enters with a tray of glasses.)*

I got my eye on him. And on you and on you and on you.

(He points to everyone except **MATTHEW.** *)*

MATTHEW. What about me?

PLOTNIK. Right. What about you?...I'm off, but watch your steps. By the end of the year, I'll have myself a murderer.

(He exits.)

MATTHEW. *(unnerved by Plotnik's warning)* Drink anyone?

DONALD. No, thank you. Bunny and I must be going. We have that appointment with the jeweler.

BUNNY. Oh, you're right. We better hurry. But it takes all the fun out of buying a diamond when someone thinks you're a murderer.

DONALD. No one who really knows you, darling, could possibly think you're capable of murder.

BUNNY. You're right! I couldn't have done it! Oh, Donald! You make me so happy. I'm ready to buy that wedding ring now!

(crossing to **JULIA***)*

Bye-bye, Mummy.

(She bends to give **JULIA** *a kiss, then whispers.)*

Oh, Mummy, remember what you told me to forget – about the pool-house? It's forgotten.

*(***DONALD** *overhears* **BUNNY** *'s remark and is noticeably puzzled.)*

Bye-bye, Daddy!

*(***BUNNY** *and* **DONALD** *exit.)*

MATTHEW. 'Bye…Now we can finally relax. We'll need this after that detective.

(He hands her a drink which **JULIA** *downs in one gulp, much to* **MATTHEW** *'s amazement. She picks up a magazine and casually leafs through it.* **MATTHEW** *waits for a reaction. Not seeing one, he produces a small bottle from his suit coat and reads the label.)*

Do not ingest. If you do, give up. Will cause vomiting, convulsions and bad breath.

(When she shows no signs of poisoning. He reads the fine print.)

To be effective, must be used by…Oh, God!

*(***MATTHEW** *slams the bottle on the desk, leaving it on top of one of* **BUNNY** *'s bridal magazines, then exits, storming out.)*

BUTTRAM. *(entering)* Ma'am?

JULIA. Yes, Buttram?

BUTTRAM. A love like ours should have lasted forever.

JULIA. Buttram. There are ways to get what you want.

BUTTRAM. Believe me, I'm doing everything I can to make it happen.

JULIA. If anyone can do it, you can. You know I'm more than happy to help. You don't have to go through with this alone.

BUTTRAM. You've already helped enough.

BUNNY. *(off)* Donald?...Donald, where are you?

(DONALD hastily exits so as not to be caught spying.)

JULIA. Buttram, darling, why don't you take the rest of the day off. You need some time to deal with this.

BUTTRAM. Thank you, ma'am...And thank you for – understanding.

(He exits. JULIA picks up the tray with the glasses as DONALD enters.)

JULIA. Donald, back so soon?

DONALD. Bunny forgot her magazines. She has marked all the pages showing what she likes. I think she said there was one over here, too.

(He crosses to the desk.)

JULIA. Help yourself.

(She exits.)

DONALD. *(finding the bottle of poison on top of the magazine)* What's this?

(He reads.)

Vomiting, convulsions?

(Suddenly, the light dawns on him.)

Love that epics are written about? There are ways to get what you want? I'm doing everything to make it happen? Good heavens! They're trying to murder Mr. Perry!

(BLACKOUT)

End of Act One

BUTTRAM. I just wanted to apologize for my little outburst this afternoon. It was entirely unprofessional of me. I feel you need an explanation.

JULIA. I don't, really, but if it would make you feel better.

BUTTRAM. Oh, it would, it would. You see, once upon a time a young apprentice butler met a beautiful woman on the street. Attired as he was in tails, and because she saw him coming down the front walk of one of the city's grandest homes, she naturally thought he was somebody rich and important. Much to his shame he allowed her to believe that…Oh, those were golden days, giddy with the glow of young love. Before that young butler knew what had happened, they were married. But the day after the wedding the young lover came clean and told her that although he did live in that house, it was in the servants' quarters. Appalled at his lies, she left him…Mrs. Perry, that young man was me. Twenty-five years ago today I was wed. Twenty-five years ago tomorrow, my heart was forever broken. All because my Estelle loved money more than me!

JULIA. Oh, my dear, I'm so sorry.

BUTTRAM. But that's only half the story. The rest is too painful.

JULIA. (*putting her arms around* **BUTTRAM** *to comfort him*) Buttram, I don't know what to say. Have you seen her since?

BUTTRAM. No, but I wish each day that I could. If I could only see her again I'd take her in my arms…

(*He takes* **JULIA** *in his arms.*)

…and tell her that our love will overcome all!…

(**DONALD** *enters unnoticed, intending to retrieve* **BUNNY**'s *magazines.*)

…A love like ours is rare upon this earth! It is the kind of love that thrills the world and gives it hope! It is the kind of love epics are made of!

JULIA. I have never heard anything so beautiful!

(**DONALD** *ducks out, embarrassed, but listens at the door.*)

ACT TWO

Scene One

(It is Halloween night at the Perry mansion. The set is the same as in Act One. The flowers are gone, and Halloween decorations festoon the room.)

(DONALD is pacing nervously.)

(He is dressed in a knight's outfit.)

DONALD. *(to himself)* I hope I can trust him…I can't do this on my own.

(PLOTNIK enters. DONALD does not recognize him.)

(PLOTNIK is dressed as Charlie Chan.)

Excuse me, sir, the bathroom is the next door over.

PLOTNIK. *(in Charlie Chan's accent)* Detective Protnik no need bathroom. Detective Protnik find what he rooking for light here.

DONALD. Detective Plotnik? Is that you?

PLOTNIK. *(dropping the accent)* The one and only.

DONALD. What a great costume. I didn't recognize you.

PLOTNIK. Isn't that the point of a costume party? And who are you supposed to be? Prince Spaghetti?

DONALD. Uh, that's Prince Valiant.

PLOTNIK. Whoever.

DONALD. Detective, I want your word you'll not tell anyone…

PLOTNIK. Mum's the word.

DONALD. I think Mrs. Perry is trying to kill her husband. And Buttram's in on it!

PLOTNIK. What put that bee in your helmet?

47

DONALD. What I've heard Buttram and Mrs. Perry say! Those "accidental" deaths around here weren't accidents. They were near misses! …I want you to protect Mr. Perry and the guests. This costume ball provides you with a cover. But you must stay incognito. No one is to know you're here. Understand?

PLOTNIK. *(as Charlie Chan)* Detective Protnik unnerstand. *(as himself again)* I've had my eye on that butler for a long time. One time I overheard him making a telephone call, and it wasn't to his Aunt Sadie in Jersey City, if you know what I mean.

DONALD. I don't. What *I'm* trying to say is – I think Mr. Perry is on to them, too. He's been spending a lot of time away from the house. Sometimes even spending evenings out. Uh oh, someone's coming, act casual.

BUNNY. *(entering)* There's my knight in shining armor. How do I look?

(She is dressed as a lady-in-waiting.)

DONALD. Wonderful, my darling.

BUNNY. Did I keep you waiting?

DONALD. But you're supposed to, you're my lady-in-waiting.

*(**DONALD** laughs. **BUNNY** is puzzled.)*

Get it? You're my lady-in-waiting?

*(**BUNNY** shakes her head, still puzzled.)*

Oh, never mind. Let's go join the guests.

BUNNY. Why is Detective Plotnik here? Has there been another death?

DONALD. How did you know he's Detective Plotnik?

BUNNY. I'm not stupid, you know.

DONALD. Well don't tell a soul he's here. It's my – surprise for midnight when we take our masks off.

BUNNY. Oh how fun! A secret. I can't wait to tell Mummy.

(She skips away, exiting.)

DONALD. *(following her, exiting)* No! No! Bunny, don't!

(**BUTTRAM** *enters, carrying a glass of champagne and a box on a tray.*)

(*He wears bunny ears and a cotton tail.*)

PLOTNIK. (*as Chan*) Good evening.

BUTTRAM. Good evening, Detective Plotnik. Are you here incognito?

PLOTNIK. (*in his own voice*) How'd you know it was me?

BUTTRAM. Lucky guess.

PLOTNIK. Well what's it to ya? Don't you have guests to wait on?

BUTTRAM. All of our usuals are either dead – or afraid they might be if they came here.

(**BUTTRAM** *puts the box on the desk.*)

PLOTNIK. What's that?

BUTTRAM. It just arrived for Mr. Perry.

(**BUTTRAM** *hands the champagne to* **PLOTNIK.**)

Mrs. Perry asked me to give this to Mr. Perry, but I can't seem to find him. Why don't you take it?

PLOTNIK. This wouldn't be a bribe or something?

BUTTRAM. I believe it's Dom Perignon.

PLOTNIK. (*downs the drink*) So, you've been working for Mrs. Perry for some time now?

BUTTRAM. Most of my adult life.

PLOTNIK. I guess you feel pretty close to her then, huh?

BUTTRAM. As close as one can be in such an arrangement.

PLOTNIK. I see. Just what do you do for Mrs. Perry?

BUTTRAM. Why, I serve her needs as best I can. That's what I'm paid for.

PLOTNIK. Oh, I see. She has to pay ya, huh? And just what does Mr. Perry think about that?

BUTTRAM. If I didn't attend to Mrs. Perry's needs, he'd have to, and those are things he'd rather not be bothered with. Why, I'm not even sure he'd know how to do half the things I do for Mrs. Perry.

PLOTNIK. I see.

BUTTRAM. Detective, as long as we're having such a frank discussion, I was wondering if you might be able to help me out.

PLOTNIK. What is it?

BUTTRAM. Well, it's a very personal matter, and it's not strictly police work.

PLOTNIK. Like what we've just been talking about?

BUTTRAM. Precisely. It has to do with a family matter.

PLOTNIK. A family you might like to become a part of?

BUTTRAM. Why, Detective, you surprise me with your perception.

PLOTNIK. *That's* what I'm paid for.

BUTTRAM. Yes, of course. Well, the thing is, I need to have something of a delicate nature done.

PLOTNIK. Done, eh?

BUTTRAM. Yes. I've tried on my own, but haven't had much luck doing it myself. You seem to be the perfect choice. As a police officer you have access to things most people can't get legally, if you know what I mean. And I have some money that I've, uh, saved, and I'd be willing to pay you quite well.

PLOTNIK. Oh you would, would you? Well, I don't go in for that kind of work, buster.

BUTTRAM. You don't?

PLOTNIK. No, penguin. I'm here to catch a killer and I smell him right now and he stinks!

BUTTRAM. I think that might be the roast duck. Cook was trying out a new recipe. Not very successfully, I'm afraid...But it hardly matters, since there are no guests left to eat it.

PLOTNIK. And just whose fault is that, huh, bub?

BUTTRAM. Like you said, Detective, that's what you're paid to find out. But have you noticed that since you've been on the case, there haven't been any more "accidents?"

PLOTNIK. Hey, now that you mention it. I guess I've got that killer on the run.

BUTTRAM. I'm sure you do.

PLOTNIK. He's probably just wondering when I'll strike.

BUTTRAM. I'm sure that's it.

PLOTNIK. He's probably about ready to confess.

BUTTRAM. Undoubtedly.

PLOTNIK. Well?

BUTTRAM. Well – I'd better attend to my duties.

*(He exits. **MATTHEW** enters.)*

*(**MATTHEW** is dressed like the Big Bad Wolf after he ate Granny – nightgown, night cap, furry hands and legs, etc.)*

MATTHEW. Plotnik, what are you doing here?

PLOTNIK. I must have the worst costume ever.

*(sizing up **MATTHEW**)*

Well, second worst.

(as Chan)

Protnik is guest of Number One son, Donald. And it took some doing to be here tonight. Halloween is a busy time for criminals.

MATTHEW. Really? I didn't know that.

PLOTNIK. That's why I'm the detective and you're…what the hell are you, anyway?

MATTHEW. The Big Bad Wolf.

PLOTNIK. You should have eaten that costume.

MATTHEW. Oh good. My package has arrived.

*(He starts to open it, then, remembering **PLOTNIK**, hesitates.)*

Oh, Detective, why don't you go and join the party. Have yourself a good time.

PLOTNIK. *(starting to leave, then stopping)* Hey, wait a minute. I'm not here to have a good time.

MATTHEW. Then why are you here?

PLOTNIK. I'm here to catch a killer. And he may strike tonight.

MATTHEW. Oh, really? Well, run along then…Oh, would you please tell my wife I'd like to see her?

PLOTNIK. I might.

(PLOTNIK exits. MATTHEW opens the package, which contains an African blowgun. He takes a dart out of the box and blows it across the room. Gleefully, he opens a tiny vial and dips a dart in it, then places it in the blower and waits. PLOTNIK reenters. MATTHEW sucks the dart back into his mouth when he realizes the person entering is not his wife.)

Your old lady's coming soon. Say, that champagne doesn't have enough of a kick, where's the scotch?

MATTHEW. Ask Buttram.

(PLOTNIK exits. MATTHEW fishes the dart out of his mouth and reloads – then readies himself just as PLOT-NIK reenters.)

PLOTNIK. Your man says the scotch is in…

(PLOTNIK never finishes the sentence because MAT-THEW nails him with a blow dart before realizing he is not JULIA. PLOTNIK slumps to the floor in the center of the stage. MATTHEW is horrified.)

JULIA. *(entering)* You know, dear, with as few guests as we have, we can't keep sneaking off to…

(spotting PLOTNIK)

Oh my God. Who have you killed now?

(JULIA is dressed as Little Red Riding Hood.)

MATTHEW. It wasn't my fault. I thought it was you and I blew it, but it wasn't you. It was him!

JULIA. You blew it all right.

(She leans over to peer at the body.)

What's Plotnik doing here?

MATTHEW. Donald invited him.

JULIA. Really, Matthew, this murdering is developing into a very bad habit. Where did you get that thing anyway?

MATTHEW. Bentworth Bartley is in Africa. I asked him to send me something.

JULIA. I knew you and your silly ideas would wind up hurting someone for real some day.

(*She checks* **PLOTNIK**'s *pulse and realizes he's not dead.*)

Why Matthew, he's not...

MATTHEW. Not what?

JULIA. *(seeing her opportunity to toy with* **MATTHEW**) Breathing, dear. He's not breathing.

MATTHEW. That's what happens when one dies.

JULIA. How are you going to explain to the police that you killed one of their detectives with an African blow gun?

MATTHEW. I'll tell them it was an accident. I was aiming for you and he walked in.

JULIA. That's brilliant.

MATTHEW. It's not like I planned this.

JULIA. Pipe down, Matthew, we've a houseful of, well, we've got a couple of people in the other room, and we don't want them to catch on...Just calm down. We've got to think.

MATTHEW. Think? How am I going to think? I just killed a man and you expect me to think?

JULIA. Oh, really, Matthew, get hold of yourself. It's not like you've never murdered anyone before. You've been doing it all year.

MATTHEW. That's true...We could just leave him here.

JULIA. No, we couldn't do that.

MATTHEW. Why not? Bentworth assured me the poison was untraceable. It'll look like Plotnik had a heart attack or something.

JULIA. But we can't just leave him lying on the floor.

MATTHEW. You're right. Let's sit him up on the sofa.

(*With great effort they maneuver* **PLOTNIK** *onto the sofa, and into a seated position.*)

JULIA. (*stepping back, taking a moment to examine the hulk on the sofa*) He doesn't look natural. He looks…dead.

(**MATTHEW** *crosses* **PLOTNIK***'s legs, and gives him a magazine, then stands back to admire his work.* **PLOTNIK** *falls to his side.* **MATTHEW** *pushes him back upright, wedging some pillows to brace him.*)

MATTHEW. There. Now let's get the hell out of here.

JULIA. (*pouring* **MATTHEW** *a drink*) First, collect yourself. We have guests to entertain. This should calm your nerves.

MATTHEW. No, not from that decanter.

JULIA. Why not?…You haven't put something in it for me, have you?

MATTHEW. Don't be absurd. It's just that this is the cheap stuff I put out for the guests.

(**DONALD** *enters unnoticed.*)

JULIA. (*disgusted*) Oh, drink up. It won't kill you.

MATTHEW. (*taking a small sip, then grimacing*) Aughhh!

DONALD. (*crossing quickly to* **MATTHEW** *and spilling the drink*) Oh! How clumsy of me.

JULIA. Oh, that's all right, Donald. I'll get a towel to clean up this mess.

(**JULIA** *exits.*)

DONALD. Are you all right, sir?

MATTHEW. What? Oh, yes. Quite all right. I just feel like I'm dying, that's all.

DONALD. You mean – you think it's the scotch?

MATTHEW. Of course it's the scotch.

DONALD. Perhaps you should see a doctor?

MATTHEW. A doctor? Don't be absurd. I'll get over it. It's not like I haven't had a taste of this before.

DONALD. You mean – you know about the other times?

MATTHEW. *(as if* **DONALD** *is a dolt)* Of course I know. How could I not know?

DONALD. And still you continue on. How – noble of you.

JULIA. *(entering with a towel)* Here we are.

(She begins drying **MATTHEW** *with the towel.)*

MATTHEW. *(to* **JULIA***)* I think Donald and Bunny are more evenly matched than we thought.

DONALD. By the way, your guests were asking for you out there, sir.

MATTHEW. Oh. Okay. Let's all go together.

*(***MATTHEW** *and* **JULIA** *check on the propped-up* **PLOT-NIK**. *No one moves.)*

DONALD. *(to* **PLOTNIK***)* Are you coming, sir?

JULIA. We were going to leave the detective alone here – to recover.

DONALD. You know who that is?

MATTHEW. Charlie Chan, right? Okay, now let's go.

(No one moves.)

DONALD. What do you mean "recover?"

JULIA. I gave him a drink and he just – passed out.

DONALD. I think I'll try to revive him.

JULIA. But Bunny is so lost at a party without you. Just let him sleep it off.

MATTHEW. Right. Let's go.

(No one moves.)

DONALD. So he's been asleep while you two were here together? So you two weren't really alone?

MATTHEW. That's right. Now, can we please all go to the party?

(They exit.)

DONALD. *(off)* I'll catch up after I hit the bathroom.

*(***DONALD** *quickly reenters, crossing to* **PLOTNIK**.*)*

You fool. Didn't you see she was trying to poison him? Didn't you? Huh?

(He prods **PLOTNIK**.*)*

You're not faking! You are drunk! Well isn't that just fine. I bring you here to protect Bunny's father, and you wind up drinking on the job.

*(***PLOTNIK*** *falls over.)*

Now look at you. Up you go.

(He sits **PLOTNIK** *up.)*

Man, you're heavy, like dead weight.

(He sits next to **PLOTNIK** *on the couch.)*

You know, there aren't too many guests today. Bunny says her parents' friends don't come around here anymore. Can't say as I blame them. Any one of them could be the next "accident." Gee, for all I know, I could be her next victim. Or you. But look at you! You already look dead. Come on, wake up, Plotnik. You've got work to do. Come on…

*(***PLOTNIK*** *falls over.)*

Plotnik?…Plotnik? Oh my God. You *are* dead. She got you, too. What am I going to do? I've got to hide this from Bunny. She can't know her mother is Lucretia Borgia. What am I saying? Even Lucretia didn't have the body count Mrs. Perry has.

JULIA. *(entering)* Oh, Donald, I didn't know you had come back here. How's our detective? Has he recovered yet?

DONALD. Recovered yet? What are you talking about?

JULIA. Has he awakened from his big sleep?

DONALD. Oh, so that's the way you want to play it, eh?

JULIA. Play what?

DONALD. I've got your number, lady.

JULIA. I think you've been palling with Plotnik too long.

DONALD. For Bunny's sake, I'll pretend I don't know what's been going on. I'll leave it up to you to do the honorable thing.

JULIA. I really don't know what…

BUNNY. *(entering, her mild intoxication immediately evident)* Oh, there you are, Donald. I've been looking everywhere for you. Hi again, Detective Plotnik.

(calling louder when hearing no response)

I said, "Hello, Detective Plotnik!"

(After an uncertain pause, DONALD, *from behind, raises* PLOTNIK*'s arm and waves it.)*

Are you enjoying the party?

*(*DONALD *nods* PLOTNIK*'s head.)*

Not very talkative today, is he?

JULIA. I'm afraid our Detective Plotnik is dead drunk.

DONALD. Good choice of words, Mrs. Perry. Very ironic, wouldn't you say?

JULIA. Donald, what are you getting at?

*(*DONALD *pulls* JULIA *aside.* BUNNY *sits next to* PLOTNIK *and begins a one-way conversation with him.)*

DONALD. *(whispering so* BUNNY *can't hear)* You know that poison was intended for someone else.

JULIA. You know about that?

DONALD. Of course I know. I've got eyes, and I've seen quite a lot in the past few months.

JULIA. Please don't let on to Mr. Perry that you know.

DONALD. You're amazing, Mrs. Perry.

JULIA. And don't worry about Plotnik here. He never knew what hit him.

DONALD. Don't worry? You've got a heart of stone, lady… I'm going to get Bunny and go into the party, and act as if I don't know what happened here…So you'd better do something about this!…Bunny?

BUNNY. *(still blithely talking to* PLOTNIK*)* I'm sure you see what I mean.

DONALD. Bunny, let's go.

BUNNY. Okay, Donald.

> *(to* **PLOTNIK***)*

> We'll finish this later.

JULIA. Bunny, and I mean this, no more punch for you.

BUNNY. But Mummy, you know I don't drink.

JULIA. Thank God I do.

DONALD. Come on, Bunny.

> *(***DONALD*** and* **BUNNY** *exit.)*

JULIA. *(checking* **PLOTNIK***)* I hope you're not out much longer. This night couldn't get much stranger.

BUTTRAM. *(entering)* Mrs. Perry, I know this may not be the best time, but I need to unburden myself.

JULIA. *(resignedly)* What is it, Buttram?

BUTTRAM. *(pointing to* **PLOTNIK***)* What about…

JULIA. Don't worry. He can't hear a thing.

BUTTRAM. Do you remember when I told you this summer about my wife?

JULIA. Yes.

BUTTRAM. I didn't tell you the whole story.

JULIA. I'm not sure I want to hear this.

BUTTRAM. But you must ma'am. Please. You see, a few months after my wife left I received a telephone call. It was from a doctor saying I owed him money.

JULIA. How unusual.

BUTTRAM. Well, I found it strange, you see, because I had never been to that particular doctor. When I inquired, I was told it was my wife's bill – for a pregnancy test.

JULIA. You don't mean…?

BUTTRAM. Yes. The rabbit died.

JULIA. You're a father, Buttram?

BUTTRAM. The fact is, I don't know if I am a father or not. I've tried to search on my own, but to no avail. I even hired a private detective, but all he did was take my money.

(He breaks down crying, embracing JULIA. DONALD *enters on the veranda, and opens the door a crack to eavesdrop.)*

JULIA. *(holding* BUTTRAM *by the shoulders, bracing him)* There, there, Buttram. Everything will work out. You know that I want the very the best for you.

MATTHEW. *(entering, very nervous)* What are you doing in here, Buttram? Don't you know we have a party going on?

(aside, to JULIA*)*

Get him out of here, now. We don't want him catching on.

JULIA. Stay as nonchalant as you seem, and not even Miss Jane Marple would catch on. Come on, Buttram.

*(*JULIA *and* BUTTRAM *exit.)*

MATTHEW. Damn. He's still dead.

(Dejected, he sits next to PLOTNIK *on the couch.* DONALD *enters.)*

MATTHEW. Oh, hello, Donald. Ah, just having a chat with Detective Plotnik here. Weren't we?

*(*MATTHEW *nods* PLOTNIK*'s head.)*

DONALD. Don't bother, Mr. Perry. I know what's happened to him.

MATTHEW. You do? How?

DONALD. I figured it out.

MATTHEW. You figured it out? My little Bunny's got herself a genius after all. Well, let's put those brains to good use and figure out what we're going to do with the body.

DONALD. I think we should call the police.

MATTHEW. The police? What kind of son-in-law-to-be are you?

DONALD. The best kind, I should hope. After all, I've seen what's been going on around here. I haven't said a word to anybody. I've wanted to spare Bunny any pain.

MATTHEW. I'm sure Bunny is feeling no pain.

DONALD. I mean, what would she think if she knew you were involved in a murder plot? That your wife…

MATTHEW. *(interrupting)* Yes, yes. We needn't dwell on the past.

DONALD. The past? What about Plotnik here?

MATTHEW. Poisoned by mistake. So you see, it wasn't intentional. Couldn't we just roll him up in the carpet or something and take him to the dump?

DONALD. That's very noble of you, sir. But I don't know.

MATTHEW. For Bunny's sake?

DONALD. All right. Just never let her know. She'll be crushed.

MATTHEW. Don't worry. She'll never hear it from me.

(They move the couch with much difficulty and roll **PLOTNIK** *up in the rug.)*

Boy, you're going to make a great son-in-law. I'll get the car and back it up here. You get our coats. And we better get out of these costumes.

(They exit. The carpet starts to shake – slowly **PLOTNIK** *unrolls himself, then sits up.)*

PLOTNIK. Ooooo…

(He shakes his head a few times, then stands, and staggers to and collapses onto the desk chair, swiveling it so his back is to the door.)

DONALD. *(entering)* I'm ready, sir…

PLOTNIK. *(interrupting)* Ooooooo…

DONALD. *(not able to pinpoint the source of the sound)* Mr. Perry, is that you?

PLOTNIK. *(sounding like a ghost)* Ooooooo…

DONALD. *(frightened)* Whoooo?

(He checks out the carpet and discovers it is empty.)

PLOTNIK. *(swiveling around, seeing* **DONALD***)* Ohhhh…

DONALD. *(seeing* **PLOTNIK***)* Oh!…You're…you're not dead anymore?

PLOTNIK. *(rubbing his head)* That's debatable.

DONALD. Mrs. Perry tried to kill you. She as much as admitted it to me.

PLOTNIK. *(as Chan)* So, rady in red and penguin tly kill me, too. Must have been poisoned dlink. Soon rearn they pick on wrong Protnik – uh – Plotnik.

DONALD. What's your plan?

PLOTNIK. *(as Chan)* Pran?

DONALD. You do have a plan?

PLOTNIK. Me have no pran.

DONALD. *(shaking* **PLOTNIK***)* Snap out of it, man. I see I'll have to come up with a pran – *plan* – of my own...Plotnik, we're going to let Mrs. Perry think she succeeded in killing you...Then you can spy on her and Buttram and collect incriminating evidence...So don't let Mr. Perry or anyone else know you're still alive. Agreed?

PLOTNIK. Agreed.

DONALD. Good, now sneak out the back way. Mr. Perry will be back any minute.

*(***PLOTNIK*** exits, still a bit wobbly.)*

MATTHEW. *(entering from the veranda)* Hurry up, Donald.

(crossing to the carpet)

Okay, you get his fee...Where the hell is he?

DONALD. I have absolutely no idea.

MATTHEW. Well, he didn't just get up and walk away now, did he?

DONALD. Of course not.

MATTHEW. Maybe Julia...

DONALD. And Buttram?

MATTHEW. *(thoughtfully)* Do you really think she would do that for my sake?

DONALD. For your sake? I swear, Mr. Perry, you're a saint. A living saint!

(DIMOUT)

End of Scene One

(With minimal time lapse between scenes, stagehands, dressed as maids and houseboys, enter to remove the Halloween decorations, and replace them with New Year's Eve decorations.)

(FADE IN to:)

Scene Two

(It is mid-evening on New Year's Eve at the Perry mansion.)

*(**DONALD** and **MATTHEW** are seated, conversing.)*

*(**MATTHEW** and **DONALD** wear tuxedos.)*

MATTHEW. Donald, my boy. By this time tomorrow you'll be my son-in-law!

DONALD. Yes, sir. I've been meaning to talk to you about that, but you've been gone so much I haven't had the chance...Where have you been lately?

MATTHEW. *(evasively)* This whole house has been taken over by your wedding – florists, dresses, planning consultants – sometimes a man just has to get away and spend time with other men, discussing men things... So I stayed at the club for a few nights. Nothing too exciting.

DONALD. I see. I wanted to warn you that something unpleasant might happen tonight.

MATTHEW. *(with an air of nonchalance that surprises **DONALD**)* Well, thank you my boy, now why don't you run along and see how Bunny's doing?

DONALD. Bunny will be down in a minute, I just spoke to her.

MATTHEW. *(trying to get rid of **DONALD**)* Oh, well, then, why don't you run and get yourself a drink of scotch.

DONALD. I never touch the stuff.

MATTHEW. You're not supposed to touch it. You drink it... Now, why don't you be a good boy and go fetch Mrs. Perry for me.

DONALD. Sure thing.

(When **DONALD** *starts to exit,* **MATTHEW** *picks up a cinder block he had hidden.)*

DONALD. *(suddenly turning back)* Oh, sir?

*(***MATTHEW** *drops the cinder block on his own foot.)*

MATTHEW. *(trying to conceal the pain)* Yes?

DONALD. I'm so very happy that I'm becoming a member of your family. Even with all the trouble with your wife, you know...It's inspiring to see the kind of love you hold for her – even after everything that's happened.

MATTHEW. Great. Now go get my wife.

DONALD. Yes sir.

(He exits. **MATTHEW** *places the cinder block above the door, positioned so that it will fall on the head of the next person to open the door. Then he crosses to obtain a syringe and a vial from a drawer.)*

MATTHEW. Now the poison.

(He injects a bottle of wine through the cork.)

Now the antidote.

(He drinks from another vial.)

And, of course, the *pièce de résistance* is already set. There's no escaping tonight. I think.

(He paces, wondering where **JULIA** *is, then, yelling through the closed door:)*

Julia! Julia?...Where in the hell is she?

(He paces, then, very upset, he goes to the door and flings it open, narrowly avoiding being smashed by the cinder block.)

JULIA. *(entering and stepping over the cinder block)* Nice try. Are we going to make our New Year's resolutions, or will I be dead by the stroke of midnight?

MATTHEW. Julia, I wish you'd stop talking like that.

JULIA. Well I should know so I can come up with a good resolution. I kept last year's quite well.

MATTHEW. There's still a few hours left. Glass of wine?

JULIA. Certainly.

> (**MATTHEW** *starts to open the wine, but he's having trouble.*)

> You know, Matthew, this past year has been rather fun, wouldn't you say? Oh, I don't mean all the deaths of course, or you being gone all the time, what I mean is…well, it's not every day one has to avoid murder attempts. At first it was tedious, but then it became exciting….It's made me think of you in an entirely new way.

MATTHEW. It's made me think of you in a new way, too, dear.

> (*His struggles with the wine bottle end as he breaks the cork.*)

JULIA. Having trouble?

MATTHEW. I broke the cork.

JULIA. What a shame. And you probably poisoned it, too, didn't you?

MATTHEW. Yes.

JULIA. Syringe through the cork?

MATTHEW. Yes.

JULIA. You know what, darling? If you still really *want* to kill me, I'll let you.

MATTHEW. You'll what?

JULIA. I'll let you kill me. I've kept my resolution. I'll help you keep yours. Go ahead, kill me.

MATTHEW. Really?

JULIA. Really.

> (*She sprawls, lying limp on the couch.*)

MATTHEW. Oh, Julia, you're the nicest woman alive.

JULIA. Not for long. Okay, get this over with.

MATTHEW. Okay.

> (*He stands above her, hands reaching to strangle, but he can't. He gets a pillow to smother her but again, he*

can't. He gets a letter opener, stands over her, and aims for her heart. He finds he can't kill her, and he collapses shamefully onto the couch.)

I can't do it. I just can't do it.

JULIA. Oh, don't despair, you've still got a few hours. Maybe you'll get the nerve up by midnight.

MATTHEW. No. I won't get the nerve up. In fact I'd given up all ideas of killing you long ago.

JULIA. Are you saying…

MATTHEW. Yes.

JULIA. But why? You were so, ah, dead set on it.

MATTHEW. It's a long story.

JULIA. Go ahead. I've got plenty of time, now.

MATTHEW. I don't quite remember when – but I realized that I'd never get away with killing you, and I didn't want to spend the rest of my life in jail…You see, I have a special reason for not wanting to be locked up.

JULIA. What *special* reason?

MATTHEW. The truth is – I've fallen in love.

JULIA. You what?

MATTHEW. I've fallen in love. I don't know when it happened, but it's true. I've fallen in love and I can't live without her. That's why I can't kill you.

JULIA. Is that why you've been spending so much time away from the house? You have another woman?…What's she like? Probably blonde with an IQ no higher than her age, right? With a waistline no bigger than your thigh, and supple breasts that still stand at attention… Oh, Matthew, how could you? After all we've been through.

BUTTRAM. *(entering)* Excuse me. I'm sorry to interrupt, but the Buffingtons just called and canceled for this evening.

JULIA. Then there won't be any guests at all tonight.

BUTTRAM. It seems everyone's afraid of ending this year the way Fifi ended last year.

JULIA. Oh dear, and tomorrow there will hardly be any guests at Bunny's wedding.

BUNNY. *(entering)* There isn't going to be any wedding tomorrow. I've called it off. I just have to tell Donald.

MATTHEW. Called it off? Why?

JULIA. I thought you loved Donald.

BUNNY. I do, but what good is that, if no one's going to see me in my wedding dress or give us presents?

MATTHEW. Darling, there's more to a marriage than a wedding dress and presents.

BUNNY. Like what?

JULIA. *(as much to* **MATTHEW,** *as to* **BUNNY***)* Like knowing what's important. Like love. And commitment.

BUNNY. Yeah, yeah, I know all that, but I still want people to see me in my dress. Oh, I guess I'll still marry him. But I'll do it in my bathrobe and curlers since no one's going to see me anyway. I'm going upstairs to cry. Wake me tomorrow when the preacher gets here.

BUTTRAM. Bunny, dear, before you go…

BUNNY. Yes, Buttram?

BUTTRAM. I just wanted to let you know how happy I am that you've found someone special, and how proud I am of the beautiful young woman you've become…All those comments I've made over the years about, oh, your elevator not going all the way to the top were… well, I didn't mean all of them.

BUNNY. It's okay, Buttram. The ones you meant were over my head anyway.

BUTTRAM. I'm sure. It's just that, I was taught the best butlers said such things.

BUNNY. I understand – I think.

BUTTRAM. Nonetheless, I want you to know I consider you my family, and because I have no child of my own…

(with a sob)

…that I can find – I'd like to give you this

(He presents a small box.)

BUNNY. *(grabbing the box, delighted)* It's a present!

(She opens it.)

Why it's…it's – a cufflink.

BUTTRAM. It's one of a pair of cuff links given to me by my wife on our wedding day. I had the jeweler remount it and put it on a chain…I hope you have more luck in marriage than I had.

BUNNY. Buttram, this is so beautiful. I don't know how to thank you.

BUTTRAM. Your smile is thanks enough. And now, I have an announcement for all of you.

MATTHEW. Announcement? What is it, Buttram?

BUTTRAM. It's a four-letter word that starts with "Q" and means leave.

MATTHEW. Oh, don't tell me!…Don't tell me!…How many letters again?

JULIA. I think what Buttram is saying is that he's going to quit.

BUTTRAM. It was a difficult decision, but I've decided it's time to move on.

MATTHEW. But you can't go. You're like part of the family.

BUTTRAM. Thank you, but I feel I must go. You see, I've been doing some soul-searching and I decided that while I'm an exceptionally patient butler, it's time to do something else. I'm starting my own company.

JULIA & MATTHEW. Your own company?

BUTTRAM. I'm going to be a financial adviser.

JULIA. A financial adviser? Where did you get the experience for that?

MATTHEW. And where did you get the money?

(DONALD and PLOTNIK enter. PLOTNIK grabs BUT-TRAM.)

PLOTNIK. We've got you now, jack.

BUNNY. So Buttram does have a first name!

MATTHEW. Plotnik! I thought you were…were…

PLOTNIK. Dead, did ya? Well, someone in this room thought they'd done the trick. And I know just who.

DONALD. Bunny, please leave. You don't want to hear this.

BUNNY. What are you talking about? Donald, what's the matter?

DONALD. I'm trying to protect you. Please go.

BUNNY. But I want to stay.

DONALD. Fine, then. But we have some terrible news.

BUNNY. Maybe I don't want to stay.

MATTHEW. Terrible news? What about?

DONALD. Crimes of the worst sort going on in this house. Crimes of deceit and betrayal. Crimes perpetrated by…

MATTHEW & BUTTRAM. *(talling to their knees in unison – pleading jointly)* Oh, please, have mercy on me! I'm so sorry. I didn't mean to…

(**MATTHEW** *and* **BUTTRAM** *look at each other in amazement.*)

MATTHEW. This is *my* confession, if you don't mind, Buttram.

BUTTRAM. *(rising)* As you wish, sir.

MATTHEW. Please, have mercy on me – I'm so sorry. I didn't mean to kill them.

PLOTNIK. What the hell are you blubbering about?

MATTHEW. I killed them. I killed them all. I am responsible.

PLOTNIK. You're saying you are responsible for the deaths around here?

MATTHEW. Yes, but please have mercy on me. I didn't mean to kill them. I was trying to kill my wife.

PLOTNIK. That's a reasonable defense.

JULIA. Oh get up, Matthew. You had nothing to do with those deaths.

DONALD. No, you didn't.

JULIA. See? Donald knows.

DONALD. Yes, I do know. It was your wife!

JULIA. What?

MATTHEW. Julia! You killed all your friends?

JULIA. Don't be silly. The gardener wasn't my friend.

DONALD. Mr. Perry has been protecting you all along.

JULIA. *He* has been protecting *me*? Oh, that's rich.

DONALD. Do you deny having an affair with Buttram?

BUNNY. Mummy!

MATTHEW. Julia! I thought you'd given up that resolution.

BUTTRAM. I assure you that Mrs. Perry and I have never…

DONALD. But I caught you in here embracing her – confessing your love to her.

MATTHEW. Is that true, Julia?

JULIA. What if it were? You have your new love, why can't I have – Buttram?

BUNNY. *(distressed)* Oh, Mummy!

DONALD. Do you deny putting poison into your husband's drink?

(**JULIA** *looks askance at* **MATTHEW.**)

MATTHEW. *(sheepishly)* I put the poison in the scotch.

PLOTNIK. You slipped a mickey into your own booze? Hey, what gives?

(pause – a slow take)

Is that what happened to me Halloween night?

MATTHEW. I'm afraid I poisoned you by accident, too, Plotnik. No offense.

DONALD. You tried to kill the detective, too?

MATTHEW. I said it was an accident. I never wanted to kill anybody – except Julia.

(falling to his knees)

I killed them all! I'm so sorry.

JULIA. Get up, Matthew. You didn't kill any of them. They were accidents.

MATTHEW. What do you mean accidents? I poisoned the tea and the Women's Garden Club drank it.

JULIA. No they didn't. I don't know why I'm helping you. You deserve to rot. The gardener mistook the teapot for the insecticide container. He poured the poisoned tea on the rose bushes. Making the same mistake, he poured the insecticide into the tea cups. Thank God I drink coffee.

MATTHEW. But what about the gardener himself? I rigged the statue to fall on you.

JULIA. Full of grief at killing all those ladies, the gardener pulled the statue over on himself. He left a suicide note.

PLOTNIK. Hey, I never saw such a note.

JULIA. *(removing a note from the desk drawer and handing it to* **PLOTNIK***)* Here it is.

MATTHEW. And Bitsy and the pool boy?

JULIA. Accidents. While Bitsy was showing Dirk her bikini wax job, she kicked the radio into the pool, electrocuting poor Dirk. And Buttram, remember the shrimp salad you served to Bitsy – the shrimp salad the cook whipped up with those little mushrooms she picked out back?

BUTTRAM. Yes?

JULIA. Deadly nightshade.

MATTHEW. You mean I didn't kill *anyone*?

JULIA. I'm afraid not.

MATTHEW. *No* one?

JULIA. Sorry, dear.

BUNNY. I wish I knew what was going on.

PLOTNIK. If *that's* rattled your little dolly brain, you better leave. There's more.

MATTHEW AND JULIA. More?

DONALD. Yes, more. Crimes of the worst sort. Crimes of deceit and betrayal. Crimes perpetrated by…

BUTTRAM. *(to* **MATTHEW***)* If I may, sir.

(falling to his knees)

Oh please, have mercy on me. I'm so sorry.

BUNNY. *(stamping her foot)* You're confusing me! Didn't Daddy already confess?

PLOTNIK. We're talking about embezzling, Missy. Money stolen from your family for more than two decades.

BUNNY. Oh, Daddy! How could you?

DONALD. Not your father, Bunny. Buttram.

MATTHEW. Buttram, what the hell are they talking about?

BUTTRAM. It's true. I've been stealing from your family for all the 23 years I've been in your service.

JULIA. We trusted you and you stole from us. Oh, why, Buttram?

MATTHEW. Never mind that…How much?

BUTTRAM. $673,418.32

MATTHEW. *(astonished)* Six hundred seventy-three thousand four hundred and eighteen dollars?

BUTTRAM. And thirty-two cents. I needed postage one day.

JULIA. There must be some mistake, Buttram.

BUTTRAM. I assure you there is no mistake, Mrs. Perry. I kept impeccable books.

MATTHEW. How did you do it, Buttram?

BUTTRAM. Your accountant gave me the idea.

MATTHEW. My accountant?

BUTTRAM. Well, you see, he told me that over the telephone, I sound an awful lot like you.

(He changes his voice to imitate **MATTHEW***'s.)*

Especially when I talk like this.

JULIA. *(with sudden realization)* I get it! Because of your child!

DONALD, BUNNY, PLOTNIK & MATTHEW. *Child?* What child?

BUNNY. I thought Buttram was a bachelor. How could he have a child?

JULIA. Thank God you're getting married…It's true, isn't it, Buttram? You spent all that money trying to find your child, didn't you?

BUTTRAM. I must confess, that was my initial intent, ma'am.

JULIA. How sweet, Buttram. I knew you wouldn't steal from us without a good reason.

BUTTRAM. Uh, well, actually, I only spent $14,066 trying to find my child.

JULIA. And the rest?

BUTTRAM. Because it was fun!

MATTHEW. Some judge of character you are, Julia.

JULIA. I suppose you're right. I trusted *you*, didn't I?

DONALD. What kind of judge of character am I? Mrs. Perry, can you ever forgive me for thinking you and this – this *butler* – had, well, an *indiscretion*?

JULIA. Don't mention it, my dear. There's only one person I know of around here who's having an indiscretion.

BUNNY. Is it contagious?

JULIA. Only among middle-aged men.

DONALD. Bunny, my darling, can you ever forgive me for thinking your mother and this…this scoundrel…this thief…this…

(He notices the necklace.)

What's this?

BUNNY. It's a necklace, silly.

DONALD. I know what it is.

BUNNY. Then why did you ask?

DONALD. I meant, where did you get it, darling?

BUNNY. Buttram gave it to me. It looks like this is going to be the only wedding present we'll get, so I hope you like it.

DONALD. Like it?…Buttram! Where did you get this?

BUTTRAM. It's one of a pair of cuff links given to me by my wife. She left me a long time ago. This and memories are all I have of her.

DONALD. Buttram, what was your wife's name?

BUTTRAM. Estelle, why?

DONALD. My mother's name was Estelle. I never knew my father. And look...

(He shows **BUTTRAM** *his cuff link.)*

I took this from my mother.

BUTTRAM. Could it be you're my...?

DONALD. Daddy!

BUTTRAM. Son!

(They embrace.)

BUNNY. God!

PLOTNIK. Let me get this straight. This place was Stiff Central this year because you wanted to ice your wife but every time you stepped up to the plate, someone took your bat away. And Loverboy here thought you and you were stepping into each other's cupboard. Again bogus. But while the penguin's rooting around in the pantry, he decides to come away with a whole handful of cabbage which he uses to find out what happened to some chick he used to pluck twenty five years ago. It turns out she laid an egghead and he's marrying your daughter?

MATTHEW. What the hell did he just say?

JULIA, BUTTRAM & DONALD. I don't know.

BUNNY. I think he's saying you're innocent, Daddy, and so is Mummy. And that Buttram is a thief and that Buttram is Donald's...

(starting to cry)

Donald's...

DONALD. *(happily)* Daddy! I've dreamed about this moment since I was able to dream, and it's finally here. I can't believe it.

BUTTRAM. Oh, this is a happy day! Let's celebrate! There's champagne in the kitchen.

PLOTNIK. Just a minute, bub. You're not going anywhere. I'm going to have to arrest you for embezzlement.

JULIA. Relax, Detective. I'm sure Buttram isn't going anywhere with the wedding coming up tomorrow. Besides, I believe Matthew and I would have to prosecute in order for you to arrest him, isn't that so?

PLOTNIK. That's right, sister.

BUNNY. Donald, is he…?

DONALD. No, dear, he's still not.

JULIA. And I don't believe my husband and I have decided on that matter yet, have we, Matthew?

MATTHEW. *We* may not have decided, but *I* have. I don't care what sentimental reason Buttram had for stealing from us – a thief is still a thief.

JULIA. As you can see, Detective, my husband and I will be discussing the matter.

PLOTNIK. I don't care, lady. The penguin ain't leaving this room without me.

JULIA. Very well, Detective. You stay here with him. Donald and I will get some champagne from the kitchen.

(**DONALD** *and* **JULIA** *exit.*)

BUNNY. Does this mean you are really Donald's daddy? Or is it like that detective calling me sister when I'm not really his sister.

BUTTRAM. It appears I really am Donald's daddy.

BUNNY. It's a good thing there won't be any guests, because I don't know if I can marry Donald now.

MATTHEW. Why not? Because he's the son of an embezzler?

BUNNY. Of course not. What kind of woman would I be if I couldn't forgive something like that?

MATTHEW. Then why can't you marry him?

BUNNY. Because he's the son of a…

(*She starts crying again.*)

…butler!

MATTHEW. So? Isn't Donald the same person he was before? The same person you've always loved?

BUNNY. Yes, but what does that matter? What would people say if they knew?

MATTHEW. They'd say you were lucky to find a young man who loves you so much and you'd be a fool to let him get away.

PLOTNIK. What's keeping them? I could use a shot.

BUTTRAM. They'll be here shortly. The champagne is right on the counter in the kitchen.

MATTHEW. The kitchen...Oh my God! I forgot!

(A massive EXPLOSION is heard off.)

*(**BUNNY** screams.)*

PLOTNIK. Another trap?

MATTHEW. I never actually thought it would work. Julia!

PLOTNIK. *(to **BUNNY** and **MATTHEW**)* Stay here. It may be ugly.

(He exits.)

BUTTRAM. My son!

*(He exits, rushing off after **PLOTNIK**.)*

MATTHEW. What have I done?

BUNNY. You killed my one true love – that's what you've done!

MATTHEW. And my one true love, too.

BUNNY. Oh, why did it matter to me that he's the son of a butler? All that matters is that he's my guy. At least he was my guy until you blew him to smithereens!

*(She sobs. **BUTTRAM** enters carrying **DONALD**. **PLOTNIK** helps **JULIA** walk. **BUNNY** rushes to **DONALD**'s side.)*

Donald, darling!

DONALD. It's all right. Thanks to my Dad. He saved my life.

BUNNY. Oh thank you, Buttram, um, Daddy. You're going to be the greatest father-in-law ever.

BUTTRAM. It was nothing. And since my son has had such a close brush with death, I want to make an announcement.

BUNNY. Not another one.

BUTTRAM. I have a little nest egg set aside.

MATTHEW. I believe that's our nest egg.

BUTTRAM. The thing is, sir, I paid back the entire amount I stole from you – with interest.

MATTHEW. How much interest?

BUTTRAM. I more than doubled your – investment.

JULIA. Buttram! You are full of surprises today.

BUTTRAM. And I have an investment portfolio worth over 4 million dollars, which I'm more than willing to share with my son – your future son-in-law.

JULIA. Under the circumstances, I think we'd be willing to let bygones be bygones. We won't be needing Detective Plotnik's services, right, Matthew?

MATTHEW. I'm not willing to let it go at that…

JULIA. But Matthew, surely…

MATTHEW. *(interrupting, speaking seriously)* I don't take what you've done lightly, Buttram. I'm planning a little trip, but when I come back – I'll be your first client in your new career as a financial adviser.

BUTTRAM. Why thank you, sir. I assure you, you won't regret it.

BUNNY. Now I'm really confused.

JULIA. Buttram is no longer a butler.

MATTHEW. And he's wealthy.

BUNNY. Oh, Donald. I'm so glad I really do love you.

MATTHEW. It's getting close to midnight. Julia, we haven't made our New Year's resolutions yet.

JULIA. I wasn't sure I would be able to.

DONALD. May I make my resolution first?

JULIA. Certainly, darling.

DONALD. I, Donald Baxter, do hereby swear that during the coming year I will do everything in my power to make my wife happy.

BUNNY. My turn. Ditto. I mean, I'm not going to make my wife happy. I don't have a wife. I mean, I will do everything in my power to make *you* happy, Donald.

BUTTRAM. My turn. I, Buttram, swear that in the coming year, my new business will make a healthy profit, and I will be a man my son – and some day my grandchildren – will be proud of.

JULIA. Detective Plotnik, how about you?

PLOTNIK. I, Detective Plotnik, swear that… I don't know what the hell is going on…. Hey, it's time to ring in this new year. That explosion didn't kill all the booze, did it?

BUTTRAM. There's more in the main bar. It's down the hall to the…

PLOTNIK. I'll find it, penguin. I'm the detective, you know. Let's go celebrate the new year.

BUNNY. And our wedding.

DONALD. And my reunion with my father.

(**PLOTNIK, BUTTRAM, BUNNY** *and* **DONALD** *exit.*)

JULIA. I suppose your resolution will be to leave me for that other woman – the one with the low IQ and the high breasts.

MATTHEW. Julia, you're wrong. The woman I love is nothing like that. She's mature. She's fun to be around. She's intelligent, and most importantly, she loves me. And over the past year I've grown to love her very much.

JULIA. How wonderful for the two of you.

MATTHEW. In fact, I intend to take her away for a long trip right after the wedding tomorrow.

JULIA. Should I clear my things out today, or can I wait until after Bunny's gone?

MATTHEW. You should probably pack today.

JULIA. I see.

MATTHEW. I just need to find out where my love wants to go.

JULIA. You sound like a schoolboy with his first crush.

MATTHEW. That's exactly how it feels...So?

JULIA. So what?

MATTHEW. So, where do you want to go?

JULIA. Where do *I* want to go?

MATTHEW. Yes, of course I meant you. Who else?

JULIA. Oh, Matthew, I didn't know. You've been away so often lately, I thought there *must* be someone else.

MATTHEW. I stayed away out of fear that one of my silly traps might actually work. Because I couln't live with myself if I couldn't live with you!

JULIA. Oh Matthew. I do love you, and I'd drift anywhere with you.

(They kiss.)

MATTHEW. Now for my resolution. I, Matthew Carter Perry the Fourth, do hereby swear that during the coming year I will do everything in my power to make my wife happy!

JULIA. Ditto.

BUTTRAM. *(entering)* Excuse me, I'm sorry to interrupt, but the champagne has been poured, and we're all waiting for you to offer the first toast.

JULIA. In a moment, Buttram.

MATTHEW. You know, my dear, I can't believe you let me think all this while that I had killed all those people.

JULIA. I was going to tell you, but you were having so much fun.

MATTHEW. I'm almost embarrassed that I didn't kill any-one...wait a minute. What about Fifi? I killed her, didn't I?

JULIA. Yes, dear, you did.

MATTHEW. Well, then. The year wasn't a total loss, was it? Come on, let's join the party.

(He exits.)

BUTTRAM. I thought Mrs. Buffington poisoned Fifi, for what she did to her fur wrap.

JULIA. She did. But don't tell Matthew. A little murder never hurt anybody.

(RAPID FADE TO BLACKOUT)

End of Play

PROPERTY PLOT

Top of Show Preset
New Year's Eve decorations adorn the room.
UL: ON THE BAR: Various filled decanters, wine bottles and bar glasses;
    A plant (which wilts in Act I –Scene 2)
DC: ON SOFA: a TV Guide and pencil.
DR: ON THE DESK: A telephone; some writing paper; several pens; a
    small hors d'oeuvre plate with a few crackers with pate

ON DR PROP TABLE:
BUTTRAM: Jeweler's eyepiece

ON UC PROP TABLE:
DONALD: A jewelry box with a diamond engagement ring

From I - 1 to I - 2:
STRIKE D:
    TV Guide and pencil
    Small hors d' oeuvre plate
    New Year's Eve decorations

SET D:
    ON COFFEE TABLE: Bridal magazines
    ON DESK: A bridal magazine
    ON COUCH: A clipboard with paper; a pen
    ON BAR: A liquor decanter with bright blue liquid (the poisoned
    decanter)
    Vases full of flowers around the room

SET U:
Vases full of flowers

ON PROP TABLE DR:
DONALD: A gold cufflink
BUTTRAM: A cardboard box containing several video tapes
MATTHeW: A small silver tray with two glasses; a third glass; a small
    medicine vial

ON PROP TABLE UC:
BUNNY: A radio with an electric cord

Intermission Preset:
STRIKE D:
- Medicine vial
- Bridal magazines
- Decanter with the blue liquid
- Vases full of flowers
- Radio

SET D:
- Halloween decorations
- On the bar: Various bar glasses, filled decanters, wine bottles and a corkscrew

STRIKE U:
- Vases full of flowers
- Plant from patio

SET U:
- Various Halloween decorations

ON PROP TABLE DR:

BUTTRAM: A tray with a glass of champagne and a box approximately 12"x4"x4" containing a blow gun, darts and a small vial.

DONALD: A fall coat

MATTHEW: A fall coat

ON PROP TABLE DL:

JULIA: A small dishtowel

From II - 1 to II - 2:

STRIKE:
- Champagne glass, blowgun box, blow dart, darts, vial; Halloween decorations, dishtowel

SET:
- New Year's Eve decorations
- Hidden on-stage: A cinder block (or brick); a syringe, two medicine vials
- On the desk: A letter opener
- In the desk drawer: A handwritten note

ON PROP TABLE DR:

BUTTRAM: Small gift-wrapped jewelry box containing necklace with cufflink (the mate to Donald's cufflink)

DONALD: Gold cufflink

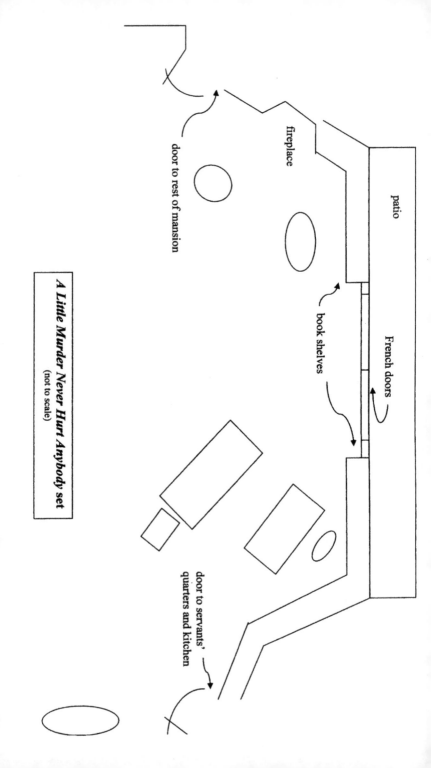

A Little Murder Never Hurt Anybody set
(not to scale)

door to rest of mansion

fireplace

patio

book shelves

French doors

door to servants' quarters and kitchen

CPSIA information can be obtained
at www.ICGtesting.com
Printed in the USA
BVHW09s2059090718
521231BV00009B/68/P